Killings

in the

Alley

By Augie Salzer

DORRANCE
PUBLISHING CO
EST. 1920
PITTSBURGH, PENNSYLVANIA 15238

Dorrance Publishing Co
585 Alpha Drive
Suite 103
Pittsburgh, PA 15238
Visit our website at *www.dorrancebookstore.com*

ISBN: 979-8-88729-136-9
EISBN: 979-8-88729-636-4

CHAPTER 1

The traffic was not the regular 8:00 a.m. rush to get to work. The heat and humidity had already reached high numbers for a typical Florida day, and tempers started to fray. An expected start for Friday the 13th.

A broken-down vehicle in the inside lane of the six-lane divided highway was causing a significant traffic jam. All the people slowing down to look at the disabled vehicle did not help the traffic flow.

Car horns of impatient drivers almost drowned out the police sirens. The cops used the shoulder to drive around the traffic, with blue and red lights flashing and sirens blaring. They pulled off Hwy. 441 and screeched to a halt in front of a broken door window of the Sumter Professional Plaza building located in The Villages.

The uniforms quickly wrapped the yellow crime scene tape around the newly planted trees in front of the building, to keep curious onlookers at a reasonable distance.

The Villages is a vast tree-lined adult retirement community that is usually very peaceful. Still, the residents do enjoy any excitement that would break up the monotony of the day. Seventy-eight different villages stretch into Lake, Sumpter, and Marion Counties, covering approximately thirty-two square miles, located in central Florida. The Villages can be found west of Daytona Beach, about fifty miles northwest of Orlando and about eighty-five miles away from Tampa. The Villages claim to be the friendliest active adult retirement community in Florida. The friendly residents lead quiet but active lives playing golf, tennis, swimming, going to parties, enjoying different hobby groups, and the more agile residents even play softball. They drive around the various communities in their customized golf carts. Decking out golf carts to make them look like a truck, a limo, or a variety of older

1

model cars takes a lot of their time and money. But when there is a disruption in their lives, they shake off their boredom and become curious onlookers. The blue and red alternating lights on the police cars were attracting a crowd. They were swarming to the flashing lights like insects drawn toward a candle flame. A replica of a red and white 1957 Chevrolet Impala golf cart led a parade of folks arriving in their fancy customized carts to find out what is happening.

Detective Lieutenant Grant Steele parks his vehicle behind the yellow tape. He sees a lot of different golf carts and wonders if there are more golf carts than actual vehicles in the area. He also notices black fingerprint powder on the outside handle and as he gets closer to the aluminum push bar inside the door. As Steele walks into the building, CSI Jack Wagner holds out a large Starbucks cup of coffee. Having a hot mug of coffee in his hand always makes Jack the best crime scene investigator in Steele's mind. He was always thinking outside the box and going above and beyond to keep the detective happy.

"I knew you could use the coffee since this is an early call, and you just don't do well in the morning. Be careful around all the glass."

"Thanks, it smells great, and it's still hot," he said as he sipped on the steaming brew. He is not a morning person and needs the caffeine to wake him up and get his brain working. Wagner quickly learned the new detective transferring in from Los Angeles six months ago was not a morning person, when he was called to an early-morning crime scene.

"Who discovered the splintered door, and did you find any prints?"

"It was an anonymous call to 9-1-1. No, the bar and handle was wiped clean. There wasn't a single print. It looks like they used a pickaxe in the corner of the glass to break the window. Also, here is the scrap of paper I found taped to the cabinets over the sink."

Wagner handed the detective a cellophane evidence bag containing the dirty note with crudely printed words "WITCH ONE" on it.

"This doesn't make any sense. I had to get up this early for no good reason. There isn't anything here," Steele mumbled to himself and knew he had to stop his new annoying habit of muttering under his breath.

Outside, the crowd was growing. One man runs toward the yellow tape wrapped around the trees in front of the building.

"You have to stay back," the uniformed cop said with his hand on his gun.

"This is my building, and I want to know what's happening."

"What's your name, and which business is yours?"

"My name is Drew Spencer, and I own the whole building. The Hands-On Physical Therapy is my business."

"It was your business that was broken into by someone. Wait here, and I'll get the detective."

Drew doesn't listen and follows the cop to his front door and sees the glass on the floor.

"I'm Lieutenant Grant Steele, a detective with the Florida Department of Law Enforcement. Come inside, but be careful around the glass. I have some questions for you. First, the uniform told me your name is Drew Spencer and that you own the building."

"Yes, sir. That's correct, but why would anyone do this? We don't keep any drugs here, and there isn't anything worth stealing."

"Mr. Spencer, are you into witchcraft?"

"No, of course not. Why are you asking?"

Steele shows the evidence bag to Spencer and tells him, "The perp left this note on the back wall with the words 'WITCH ONE' on it. Does that mean anything to you?"

"No. Why?"

"I was just trying to figure out why this note was left. So, I will take this note to the lab and check for prints. Oh, by the way, how many people work here?"

"I have another physical therapist, Chuck Vaughn. He's been with me since the beginning, and Will Hudson is a therapy assistant and co-owner of the business. I also have Rick Carr, a therapy assistant, and brothers Allen and Arthur Whyte are rehab techs."

"Thanks. I notice you have cameras. Do they work?"

"Sure. I'll get you the footage."

The uniform guarding the door gets another call and gathers the yellow tapes before he leaves. Then, with the preliminary investigation almost completed, others are allowed to enter the building.

Drew doesn't see his partner arrive as two patients carefully enter the office, and the techs take them to the treatment area. A young woman also enters the building.

"Hi, I'm Ashley Parker from the *Village Chronicle*. Can you tell me what happened?" she said to no one in particular.

"Can't you wait until the news release comes out?" Steele asks, annoyed.

He doesn't like nosy reporters because, in his opinion, they are always in the way. His job would be easier if reporters weren't allowed at crime scenes.

"I was driving by and noticed all the blue lights and cop cars, and I had to see what was going on. Of course, my readers will want to know what all the excitement is about too," she said.

While Steele deals with the intruder, Drew notices Will in the room.

"Will, glad you got here. Could you sweep up the glass before someone gets hurt?"

"That's not my job. Get one of the techs to do it."

"Oh, by the way, what's wrong with the cameras? The screens are blurred."

Will turns his back and goes to his first patient.

"Sorry, Lieutenant, it seems the cameras are not working, so I don't have any footage to give you."

"That's okay. Here's my card. If you find anything missing, give me a call. I'll get back to you if I have any questions," Lt. Steele said as he left the store.

Ashley Parker starts asking Drew some questions about his business, and if this ever happened before?

"We have been in business here for about eight years, and we have never had any problems like this before. So, this break-in is a first for us."

After getting all the information she can, Ashley leaves the building and questions the crowd, looking for a witness to the break-in. Everyone is eager to talk to the reporter to get their name in the paper, but no one claims to have seen anything. So, her story will be short with just the mention of a break-in at a local business, and the investigation is ongoing.

CHAPTER 2

Drew Spencer walks out the back of the three-unit building only to see cobwebs all over the cameras. Gray Spanish moss drips from the majestic live oak trees growing near the corners of the building and covering the cameras.

He sees Bette Thompson enjoying a rare and refreshing breeze while smoking a cigarette in the alleyway.

Drew is six foot two and dwarfs Bette at five foot four. She is wearing the beauty salon black slacks and a matching smock embroidered with the name of her salon, Cut & Curl by Bette, in the upper left corner. Bette is on the chubby side and has a bounty of bleached curls piled on her head. She has lived a hard life, and it shows on her wrinkled face, making her look older than her forty years.

"What happened in your store?" Bette asks Drew.

"I don't know. It seems somebody broke the door, but it doesn't look like anything was taken or vandalized."

"Do you think we have to be worried that they might come back?"

"I don't know, but I wouldn't think so," Drew said as he returned to his office.

A whole new security system was supposed to be installed some time ago, he remembered. He's confused about what is going on and why somebody didn't install the system? Since Will is in charge of fixing any repairs in the building, he will have to ask him about it.

The patients just kept asking questions about the broken glass until Drew finds a handyman to replace the glass in the door.

Patients arrive for their appointments, and the turmoil of the morning soon blends into the day's usual activities.

The mailman arrives as everyone takes a lunch break with their regular

Friday pizza order from Tony's next door. The men eat the gooey cheese and meat pizza and talk about the morning break-in. But, of course, they all have different opinions on why someone would go to the trouble of breaking into a place just to put a note on the wall.

"Hi, Mr. Spencer," the postman said. "I have a certified letter for you or Mr. Hudson and need a signature."

"I'll sign for it."

"Thank you, and here is the rest of your mail."

The postman gets the signature and drops a bundle of mail on the desk on his way out.

Drew searches for the letter opener, trying to figure out the secret of the thick envelope. Unfortunately, the mailman usually brings only bills and junk mail. What could this possibly be? He was not looking forward to the contents. Friday the 13th has always been bad luck for him and today was no exception.

When he was eighteen years old, both his parents died in a one-car accident on Friday the 13th. As a result, he always felt forced to take care of his ten-year-old sister, Ginger, so that the government wouldn't put her into the foster care system. Since there weren't any relatives to care for her, he felt he didn't have a choice, and he had to do the right thing. The stress of losing his parents and raising his sister has caused occasional panic attacks and incapacitating migraines for him.

Every time Friday the 13th shows up on the calendar, Drew deals with a rash of bad luck and debilitating anxiety.

I should have just stayed in bed, he thinks to himself.

Not finding the letter opener, he awkwardly tears open the bulky envelope. Several pieces of legal bond stationary explain a foreclosure procedure is in process. The stark white official pages continue explaining that Drew Spencer and co-owner William Hudson have not paid the last four mortgage payments putting their property in default. The bank is preparing to sell or auction the property within the next sixty days unless the owners take some action to eliminate their debt. Drew is confused, and his heart is racing. He looks for Will, but he's not in the building. Drew goes out the back to clear his head and enjoy the refreshing breeze. He sees Bette and Pete Rossi from the pizza place outside smoking by her back door. They are talking, and he doesn't want to be bothered with small talk, so he heads back to his office, but Pete Rossi's question stops him.

"Hi, Mr. Spencer. Bette was just telling me about this morning. I was coming to work and saw all the police cars. So, I went to have breakfast, and when I came back, the cops were gone. Will they be coming back?"

"Since nothing was taken, I doubt they'll return," Drew said.

"Okay, I was just wondering if the cops said they'd be back," Pete asked.

Drew walks back to his office and sees his partner finished with a patient. Instead of going to join in with the rest of the guys for lunch, Will heads out back to smoke.

"Will, could you come here for a minute before you go outside?"

"What do you want now?"

Drew hands him the recently received foreclosure pages.

"Could you explain this?"

Will reads the letter and rubs his hand over his balding head and neck, stalling for time.

"I don't know anything about this," he said, throwing the papers on the desk, scattering them onto the floor.

"What do you mean that you don't know anything about this. Since we started this business eight years ago, haven't you been paying the bills? That was part of our arrangement, but now you don't know what's happening?" Drew said, clenching his fists and pounding the desk. "What is wrong with this picture?"

Will turns, walks out of the office, and goes outside for his smoke break, leaving Drew standing there fuming.

CHAPTER 3

Will Hudson moved next door to Drew Spencer's house in the Spruce Creek Country Club's quiet community about ten years ago. It is a serene, quiet neighborhood about one mile west of The Villages. The cookie-cutter houses with a large Magnolia tree planted in every front yard and the same-sized lawns dominate the area. However, several homes painted with vibrant yellow, fuchsia, or bright blue help break up the neighborhood's monotony.

The two quickly became friends. At that time, Will was married and had a problem avoiding the poker table. The obsessive lure of Texas Hold'em had always been his downfall. He could smell a game anywhere and considered himself lucky to be invited to it when he had the money for a buy-in. His gambling cost him his family, wife, and job over the years. Working as a clerk in a quick money lending and check cashing company was boring. This career was not his idea of fitting his lifestyle. He didn't like working at the Fast Personal Loan Company and giving $500 to those less fortunate than he was when he was the one that needed the money to gamble.

He felt it was his wife's fault if he lost. After she filed for divorce and left, he was on a winning streak for a while.

It was at this time that Drew and Will became good buddies. They talked about possibly going into a business together. Since Will didn't like his job, and Drew didn't enjoy working for someone else, they worked on a plan to start a business. Drew was a physical therapist working for a doctor in Orlando, and he detested the hour-long drive to work each day.

Unfortunately, Drew didn't know about Will's gambling addiction. He always dreamed of owning his own business closer to home. Drew pretended to be the doctor for his younger sister's stuffed animals as a young boy. However, the family responsibilities of caring for his sister had prevented him from his dream of becoming a doctor. Instead, he was happy as a physical therapist since he enjoys helping people.

"We should get into some kind of business together," Drew said to Will ten years ago.

"That would be great, but what kind of business can we open?" Will asked.

"We could open a physical therapy clinic," he said. "You could go to the University of Florida in Orlando and become a physical therapy assistant. That's the school I went to, and I could help you with your studies. It won't be difficult for you because I will help you every step of the way."

Will didn't seem happy about the business type, but he was desperate to find something that would start making him some real money so he could continue gambling.

The two came up with a business partnership. Will could start with a small down payment since he was presently short of funds. Then, after Will began earning his way, he would use part of his salary to pay off the rest of his financial commitment.

"Since I don't like to do everyday finances, you can handle the books and do all the paperwork. We can count that job toward the payment of the amount you owe," Drew said as he mentally saw his dream come true.

It didn't take long before Will was enrolled in school and completed the work to become a physical therapy assistant. Before Will graduated from school, Drew found the perfect building for their business located right off Hwy. 441. It was about one mile from the large Epic Medical Center, with several orthopedic doctors and surgeons on staff. The location would give them many referrals from the local doctors and still have a lot of pedestrian traffic passing by their office.

Drew contacted his good friend, Chuck Vaughn, a physical therapist in New York, to join his new business venture. The two had been friends since grade school in Minnesota. Then Chuck's family moved to New York. They kept in contact with each other over the years and found they had similar interests, and both became physical therapists.

So, when Chuck talked to Drew about opening his own physical therapy business, he was happy to leave the frigid Staten Island to become a part of his good friend's business venture.

Drew was busy locating another rehab assistant and two rehab techs to staff the office. He was fortunate also to find two other businesses willing to rent the remaining offices in the three-unit concrete block building he was planning to buy.

All the commercial buildings in the area are built with a Spanish-style decor. The Spanish Colonial-styled building that he found was painted a light gray with dark gray trim and still looked good after being bleached by the hot Florida sun for the past five years. The physical therapy group is the first unit, then the Cut & Curl by Bette's beauty salon is in the middle, and Tony's Pizza parlor is at the end of the building.

Each unit is approximately 2,000 square feet with a glass front door, a large window next to the entrance, and a rear exit. In addition, there is a private office in the back of each unit right across from a bathroom.

The interior of the Hands-On Physical Therapy unit was painted a light blue-green to evoke a sense of calm and create a relaxing effect for the patients. The clinic has three treatment tables and two tables for hand therapy. A sink for patients to wash their hands is by the front door, with three cabinets above the sink to hold their supplies. There is still sufficient room for the exercise equipment needed for their patients. Their office has two small, well-worn thrift store desks facing each other with an old computer on one desk. There are some folding chairs for the guys to sit on during lunch. A dirty plaid cloth sofa from a thrift shop is against the wall with a dark brown throw over the back.

The Cut & Curl by Bette has two stations on the shop's west wall. Since the beauticians only work part-time, they are not always there. Bette's station is on the east wall opposite the front door and next to the shampoo sink. Her office has a small computer desk and chair. She also has an oversized comfortable beige leather couch covered with large pale blue pillows with matching fringe taking up most of the room. She keeps her laptop on the desk to keep track of her appointments and payments. Bette chose her favorite color of light blue paint for the walls to give off energy and warmth to her clients.

Tony's Pizza joint fills most of his unit with the ovens and prep counters. As anyone walks into the shop, the delicious smell of his famous sauce cooking is the first thing they notice. He has large, bold stripes of green, white, and red painted on his main wall to represent his Italian heritage.

Tony's office has a black leather sofa with a pillow and warm blanket for him to nap when business slows down. In addition, he has Pete Rossi for the occasional deliveries. Since most of his customers are walk-ins from the street, many others call in or order online and pick up their order. Since he only has an occasional pizza order requiring delivery, he doesn't plan to hire additional help. However, when he first opened his shop, Tony had a lot of delivery requests, and he needed to hire a delivery person.

Rossi was a young man looking for work and answered Tony's Help Wanted sign placed in his store window.

After a while, most of the population of The Villages acquired a golf cart, and it is easier for them to hop in their cart, pick up their pizza and not have to pay the delivery charges or tip the driver.

Since Rossi has been with Tony from the start, they have become close friends. Tony considers Rossi as the son he never had. Although the delivery requests have dropped, Tony will always keep Rossi on the payroll.

CHAPTER 4

Discovering his dream was slowly disappearing, Drew remained in his office, seething and running his fingers through his hair.

He is making an effort to act like everything is normal. He didn't like conflict and would do anything to avoid it. When he and his sister were young, he still vividly remembers his parent's screaming when they fought. When his Dad started to hit or grab his mother as they argued, he clearly remembers they would run and hide in the back of their closet with their hands over their ears and eyes closed tight so they couldn't hear or see them. Even today, Drew still has occasional nightmares about his parent's fights.

Drew sat at the desk and started going through the pile of mail. He was throwing away one piece of junk after another until he saw the letter from the insurance agency and another one from Barry, their accountant. His heart started to race again. He wasn't feeling well and wondered what else could be going wrong?

The insurance company sent their bill of $6,500 for the year's coverage, and it was a second notice requesting immediate payment. Their accountant's letter stated that their quarterly income taxes were past due, and Will hasn't paid them. His thoughts went to wondering how long he was taking money and how much has he taken?

Frustrated, Drew looked for Will. He had left the building, but no one knew where he went.

Drew went back to his office to lie down and calms himself with controlled breathing to avoid a horrible migraine. This technique usually helped with his anxiety. He fears losing his dream of owning his business, and he knows the stress will give him a severe migraine.

His mind began racing over the last few months, questioning why he didn't notice that something was going on but he couldn't remember anything out of the ordinary. Was he too busy to see what was happening right under his nose?

Maybe he should have noticed that the security cameras were still not installed, but he never took the time to look outside. Will claimed the cameras were purchased but Drew never followed up on their installation. He never looked for trouble as long as everything was going smoothly. Will would always answer any questions Drew asked him about the office finances.

Everything was going well for years. Will was always able to pay back the money he borrowed from the company and pay all the bills before Drew noticed anything was wrong.

But then things changed and his winnings went for significant gambling losses and high-priced escorts during the last couple of years.

Will's problems began right after his wife left him. After he was lucky enough to win $50,000 in a no-limit Texas Hold'em game. Mac, the host of the poker games, suggested as a big winner, Will might enjoy the company of Jasmine.

"Give this number a call. You will appreciate Jasmine, and she will treat you right. For a grand, she will show you a good time. She is very nice and likes big winners," Mac said as he handed him the number.

With his winnings in hand, Will is intrigued by this information and looking forward to meeting Jasmine. But first, he buys himself a gold, lucky horseshoe diamond pinky ring to celebrate his big win.

CHAPTER 5

After arguing with Drew, Will enters the rear of Bette's shop.

"Do you have a minute?" Will asks. "I have a problem."

"Sure, go into my office. I just have to finish my last lady for the day, and I will be there in ten minutes."

Bette completes the styling of her client's hair and cashes out her lady. Then she goes to her office to see Will waiting on the couch, minus most of his clothes.

He starts unbuttoning Bette's smock and removing her slacks. He pulls her to him while he kisses her neck as they lay on the couch. They caress and kiss. Two minutes later, Will is finished, gets off the couch, and dresses.

"You could have waited for me so we could finish together," she said, disappointed.

"It's all your fault. If you didn't take so long with your client, we would have had an extra ten minutes."

"Why do we always have to sneak around here? Why can't we ever go to your place? It would be much more comfortable being in a bed instead of this old couch. We would also have more time together."

"You know I live next door to Drew, and he would see your car in my driveway. He is such a stickler for doing the right thing all the time."

Although Will's divorce was finalized a while ago, he doesn't want Bette to know the divorce is final. She has already suggested she could live with him, which is not an option for Will.

Bette is upset and wants him gone.

"Just get out. I don't want to look at you now," she screamed as she finished dressing and turned her back to him.

Will leaves to go outside with his e-cigarette for a smoke.

Drew walks out back and sees Will.

"Get in here. I want to talk to you about this mess you've gotten us into." Drew wants to get everything resolved. He likes to have everything organized and nothing out of order.

Will takes his time smoking before going in to face Drew.

"Okay, Will, how did we get to the point that we are going into foreclosure?"

"Hey man, it's not my fault that we're in the hole."

"Then whose fault is it? Why haven't you been paying the bills? Where has all the money gone? Answer me," he said as the veins in his neck bulged.

After hesitating for many minutes, Will finally admits that he has a problem.

"I had a couple of card room markers that I had to pay back. So, I borrowed some money from the business until I was hot again. After that, I didn't have a choice," Will confessed.

"I can't believe you used all this money for gambling. How are we supposed to come up with the money to pay all our bills or do we just give up and lose the business we have been building for so many years?

"All right, Drew, if you just give me a couple of thousand. I know I can get it all back at the table," Will said.

"Are you out of your mind? No way you are getting any more money, and as of now, I will take care of the finances for the business. So, you just stay away from the checkbook and leave the money alone. I don't want you to have anything to do with the finances. Also, from now on, I will be taking half of your paycheck to pay back all the money you already took from the business," Drew said as he clenched his fists.

Will leaves the office, slamming the door.

Now Drew has to figure out what to do next. What can he do to save his dream? Is bankruptcy an option? He is troubled trying to figure out the next move. He doesn't want to lose everything he has built over the years, but how can he trust his partner again?

Drew sits at his desk, holding his head, and decides to call his wife, Vicky. She has always been the level-headed one in their fifteen-year marriage. He's convinced that she will know what to do to fix this mess with her positive outlook.

"Hi, hon. Do you have a few minutes? I have a real problem, and I don't know what to do. Sit down. I have some terrible news to tell you."

"Oh my. What's wrong? Are you okay?" she said concerned.

"It appears Will has been embezzling money from the business. I don't know how long this has been going on. I received foreclosure papers in the mail this afternoon for our building."

"Oh no, how did his happen? I can't believe Will would do something like this. He always seems like a nice guy. This is terrible. What are you going to do?"

"I'm not sure, but somehow I have to stop the foreclosure. I just can't lose the business I've worked so hard to build."

"Why don't you call Barry your accountant. He's pretty knowledgeable about businesses, and I'm sure he can help you. We can talk more when you get home tonight. Don't worry. Things will work out, and they always do," Vicky said with a positive attitude.

He takes his wife's advice, calls their accountant, and tells him about his problem.

"Hi, Barry, this is Drew Spencer from the Hands-On Physical Therapy, and I need your help."

"Sure, what's the problem?"

"My partner was in charge of the books, and he has used all our money for gambling. He was supposed to be paying the bills, but we are already four payments late on our mortgage, and now the bank has started foreclosure on us. You know how high our mortgage payments are, and I don't have any money to pay them. Also, our insurance bill of $6,500, which is already past due, came in the mail today. The money that we get from our patients' Medicare and the insurance companies goes into the business direct deposit, and it looks like he took it out as fast as it came in. Presently, our account only has a few hundred dollars in it, which isn't enough to cover the electric bill. I just don't know what to do," he said, talking too fast.

"First of all, take a deep breath. It appears that you are in serious trouble. Right now, it sounds like your best option would be to do a Chapter 11 filing," the accountant explains the procedure. "It stops the foreclosure process by reorganizing your debts, and it is fairly easy to do."

"Thanks, I really appreciate all your help. Oh, can you get an extension for us on our quarterly taxes too?"

"Sure, Drew, I can file for an extension for your taxes."

After talking to his wife and the accountant, he is feeling a little better. The work is finally finished for the day and Drew goes home. His whole life, he has been superstitious, and he blames his current rash of bad luck on the date.

He goes home to be with Vicky and hopefully spend some time relaxing.

"How did things go at the office?" she asks.

"I took your advice and called our accountant, and he suggested filing for a Chapter 11. He said that would stop the foreclosure, and we should be okay."

"That is great news, but what are you going to do about Will?"

"What would he do if I fired him? He has no one except us, and we can't just let him go. I already told him that we would be taking half of his pay in the future to cover the money that he stole from us. I also told him he wasn't to touch the books anymore, so he won't be able to take any more money."

"I have an idea. Why don't I go in and take care of the books for you? I like to do bookkeeping, and since I only work as a substitute high school teacher anyway, I have plenty of time to do this. So, what do you say?"

"Oh, Vicky, you are the best wife anyone could have. It's a fantastic idea. Can you start tomorrow?"

"It would be my pleasure. Now, why don't you sit and put your feet up? I'll get you a beer before I start dinner."

"That would be great. I still don't feel well, but knowing you're here to help me is great."

"What's wrong?"

"I don't know. I just don't feel well, and I'm still having night sweats."

"Okay, but don't let it go on too long. Then, if you want, I can make an appointment for you to see our doctor?" Vicky said.

"No, don't worry about it. I'm sure it's just all the stress. If I don't feel better soon, I'll go to the doctor."

"You know how I worry about you."

CHAPTER 6

When Drew and Will organized the physical therapy business, it was decided they would work Monday through Friday and have the weekends off to enjoy life.

The beauty shop works Tuesday through Saturday with evening hours to accommodate special clients. The pizza shop is open seven days a week until 11:00 p.m.

Tony is a widower and lives by himself. Now that he is alone, his whole life's passion is just to make his Italian pizza. He is content to nap on his couch when business is slow, so he doesn't have to go home to an empty house.

Saturday afternoon, Will walks in the back door of Bette's shop when the other beauticians have gone out to lunch.

"What are you doing here?" she said as she walked to her office. "I didn't think you guys worked on Saturday."

"We don't. I just came here to visit my beautiful lady and hope you have some time for me." He follows her and starts rubbing her shoulders.

She turns, and they kiss. Will starts taking off her smock and kissing her neck as they both fall on the couch. He caresses her back while kissing her. The passion rises in both of them. Will takes his time, while making sure Bette is happy this time.

"Well, that was great."

"Hope that makes up for the last time I was so rude?"

"It sure does. It was wonderful."

"Good. Hey, babe, do you think you could lend me three thousand dollars? I need to pay off a gambling debt. I'll pay you back. I promise."

"So that's why you came here today," she said, standing up and putting her clothes on. "It wasn't to see me. It was just to get my money. You haven't even paid off the last $500 I lent you. Why should I believe that you'll pay me back now?"

Will gets up and caresses Bette. "Come on, babe. I really need this."

"Why don't you get the money from Drew?"

"He's talking about filing bankruptcy or something, so he doesn't have any money. I'm desperate."

"I'm sorry. I didn't know. Why would the business go bankrupt? You always have a lot of patients in there."

"Something about the bills not being paid or something."

"You know that I don't have that kind of cash around."

"Bette, I'm in a lot of trouble and need your help. You know I love you. Don't you have about $1,500 in your cash box?"

"I already took the cash to the bank before lunch," she said.

"If you don't have the cash, can't you give me a check?"

She reluctantly gets her checkbook and starts writing the check. The brass sleigh bells on a leather strap hanging on the front doorknob announce the first client of the afternoon.

"Sit in my chair. I will be right out," Bette yells to her client.

"Why am I such a sucker for you? Here's your money. You had better pay me back this time plus the $500 you borrowed before."

"Thanks, Bette, you're a doll. You know I love you, and I will pay back every penny."

"You had better. I'm doing you a favor, but I need this money back in two months, do you understand?"

"Sure, Bette. I promise you that you'll have all the money back as soon as I can."

Will goes to his office, takes a check from the desk without recording it, and discovers $800 is still in the account. He goes to the bank to cash the checks and leaves with almost four thousand dollars. After getting home, the first thing on his agenda is to call Jasmine. Celebrating with her is necessary before he finds a new game.

The first time Will called Jasmine, she told him that her protocol keeps her clients unidentifiable.

"Everyone gets a number for their first time, and when you call for another appointment, you use the number I give you. This way, you don't have to worry about me trying to blackmail you or give your identity to the cops if they ever raid me," she explained.

"From now on, your name is John 22, and when you call, I will tell you which hotel room to meet me. I use different hotels and rooms for my protection."

With his recent cash windfall, Will calls the number he has memorized.

"Hi, Jasmine, this is John 22, and I would like to see you tonight if you're available?"

"Sure, John 22, come to the Cosmopolitan Hotel room 501 at about 6:00 p.m."

"I'll be there at six on the dot."

He spends the next several hours showering and shaving in preparation for the evening.

As Will knocks, Jasmine opens the door wearing a white silk negligee so thin that it looks like she is floating on a cloud. Her medium-length, brown hair with a reddish tint falls just past her shoulders. As she walks into the room on her stiletto heels, a waft of intoxicating perfume flows behind her.

"Jasmine, you look gorgeous as usual. Just like an angel. Let's sit down for a while so we can talk, and I can enjoy your beauty."

They sit and talk as Will tells her again about his boring life. He goes on and on about the terrible life he had in Cleveland, Ohio as a bookkeeper. He then tells her that working at the Hands-On Physical Therapy is also very dull.

"I went to Cleveland a long time ago and went to the First Energy Stadium, the home of the Cleveland Browns, and I thought it was beautiful at night," Jasmine recalled. "Did you ever go there?"

"No, I'm not into sports that much. But I wish I could take you to New York, which is an exciting city. There is a restaurant that makes the best steak you have ever eaten. I would show you the wonderful New York. The city is always full of excitement with so many different things to do. There is always something going on, not like here. I like excitement and adventure, and I know you do too."

"I'm content to live and work here. There is enough excitement for me right here."

Will continues talking. Suddenly, he takes her hand and leads her to bed.

The evening is always the same for Will. A night of talking to a brilliant, knowledgeable, and intelligent female. Then intensive lovemaking with the most beautiful woman he has ever seen ends in ecstasy and disappointment. The time is never long enough, and he doesn't like having to share Jasmine, but he doesn't know what to do about it.

"Why do I have to share you with other men? You know how much I love you and want to take you away from all of this."

"I understand, John 22, but you don't have any money. I've become accustomed to my luxurious lifestyle. You usually don't even have enough money to pay for my services, let alone take me away from here. I'm happy with my life, and I have no desire to change it. Why don't you just earn enough money, and we can have another evening together?"

Will reluctantly leaves the hotel room as his night of bliss is over. Now he is forced to go back to being ordinary Will Hudson with his uneventful life.

CHAPTER 7

Bette has been suffering from shoulder pain for almost a week before she goes to a doctor. The doctor explained that she has a torn rotator cuff and that she would need therapy to fix the problem. She deals with her pain until Wednesday afternoon then goes to Drew for help.

"Hi, Drew. It seems I need your expertise. Can I make an appointment with you to fix my shoulder?"

"Sure. What's the problem?"

"I went to the doctor, and he said my rotator cuff tendon got messed up or something. All I know is that I'm in pain and hope you can help me. So, he gave me a script." She gives him the paper.

"Your doctor wants me to do an evaluation of your shoulder. You're in luck. I just finished with my last patient, so I can see you now."

"Thanks, Drew. I really appreciate this."

"First, we'll give you some range of motion therapy using different equipment and measure the results to see any improvement after some therapy sessions. We'll start today using some resistance exercise bands and light weights. How did you manage to hurt your shoulder?"

"I'm not really sure. I think I hurt it by putting a box of supplies on the top shelf of the closet. At first, I thought it was a pulled muscle, but I knew I had to see a doctor when it didn't get better. It took me six weeks to get an appointment with a specialist. I just need you to fix it because it interferes with my work."

"No problem. We'll start you on some exercises and have you good as new in no time."

As he shows Bette several different exercises, Drew starts taking measurements to see the range of motion Bette has with her shoulder. Later Bette lies on the table as Drew continues with various workout activities. After putting ice on her shoulder for five minutes, he then rubs on the No Pain Freeze cream to relieve the workout pain.

"This ointment is a fast-acting relief from topical pain," Drew tells her while rubbing the lotion on her shoulder. "I'll have Allen give you a small sample to take home with you. Then he'll make some appointments for you before you leave. The doctor wants you to come here three times a week for four weeks. After that time, I'll send him an update on your progress, and he will tell us what the next step is for you."

"Thanks, Drew, it feels better already. I'll make the appointments and see you later."

Lt. Steele walks into the shop as Bette and another patient are leaving.

"Mr. Spencer, I want to update you on the case."

"Sure, that was my last patient. Come back to my office. Can I get you some coffee?"

"Yes, black would be good. We finally found a partial print on the note that somebody left here."

"That's great, but I thought you could find the owner of fingerprints in just a couple of hours," Drew said as he handed the mug of steaming hot coffee to the lieutenant.

"No, that only happens on TV shows. In real life, it takes a lot longer. The print belongs to Pauli Saffarino. Pauli and Anthony are twins with connections to the Italian mafia in New York City. Most Mafiosi are neither educated or well spoken. Our informants say the brothers have taken over the low-key gambling and prostitution business here outside of the Orlando area. So far, they aren't causing any trouble, so we're just keeping a close eye on them. They live and work in the Cosmopolitan Hotel."

"What would the mob want with me and my business?" Drew asked.

"Right now, we don't know the answer to that, but we're working on it. Because the note had 'WITCH ONE' written on it, I believe it could have been a mistake or mistaken identity, but keep me informed if anything else happens. We're also investigating cold case murders in the alleyways in this area over the past couple of years. So be careful when you're out at night."

"Thanks, Lieutenant. Do you think the break-ins and murders are connected?"

"No, I don't think they are, but you might want to get your cameras fixed anyway," Steele said.

"Appreciate your help. While you're here, can I talk to you about a problem?"

"Sure. How can I help?"

"My partner, Will Hudson, has taken a lot of money out of our business, and I wondered if you could do a background check on him? He told me he took the money to pay some gambling debts."

"How long has he been embezzling money from you?"

"I don't know, but it has been at least four months since it appears Will made any mortgage payments. But I won't know how much money is missing until I check the books."

"I can arrest him today if he's here."

"No, I don't want him arrested. I just want him to pay back all the money he stole from me. Also, I want to know if he has done this in the past."

"To do a background check, I will need a full name, date of birth, Social Security number, address, and his email address."

"That won't be a problem. I have all that information from when we started the business." Drew looks up the information on the computer and gives it to the lieutenant.

"I'll get back to you as soon as I have the results."

Back at the station, he heads to the Investigations Department and talks to Nancy, the department's head.

"Hey, Nancy, can you do me a favor? "

"Not another favor. You still owe me for the last one."

"If you do a rush on a background check for me, I'll take you out to dinner," he said, flirting with her.

"What, another hot dog from the Roach Coach outback? No, thank you."

"No, this time, it will be at a real restaurant complete with cloth tablecloths and everything."

"Oh, I can't wait. Okay, give me the info, and let me get to work. I will have the information for you in no time. Then you can make the reservation at a place with tablecloths."

CHAPTER 8

Drew walks outside of the building toward his car on his way home and trips over a garbage bag left next to his back door. The immediate intense pain in his left ankle causes him difficulty in getting up. While trying to stand, he thinks maybe it's time to install a light out here so we can see in the dark.

"So, why would anyone leave a bag right by the door? Great, just what I need more lousy luck," Drew said to himself.

He figures the first incident was the glass door breaking, and the second was Will taking all the money and trying to destroy the business. Hurting his ankle makes the third occurrence.

Since superstitious people claim all lousy luck happens in threes, Drew hopes the bad luck is now over. He feels relaxed for the first time in days as he throws the garbage bag in the dumpster. He then hobbles over to the Fast Care medical office down the street to get his sore ankle checked by a doctor. He's confident that everything will be fine now and return to normal.

He tells the doctor about the night sweats he has been having the last few weeks as he waits for the radiologist to take a series of x-rays of his ankle.

The doctor looks over the x-rays and explains that the results show it is just a simple sprain with no broken bones. The nurse then wraps his ankle with an elastic bandage. Next, Drew receives a set of crutches and directions on how to care for his ankle. Then the doctor tells him he has to stay off his foot for a few days to a week, and he should be as good as new. He is also told to keep his foot elevated so it doesn't swell. After that, he should see his family doctor for his night sweats and any future problems with his ankle.

The following day, he arrives at work using the new crutches and sees Bette unlocking her door.

"What happened to you?" she asks as she opens his door for him.

"Last night, I tripped over a garbage bag someone left by my back door. I'm thinking of installing lights at our back doors, so this won't happen to anyone else."

"That sounds like a great idea. It does get dark out here at night, and we don't want someone else to get hurt, especially me," Bette said.

"I'll try to find someone to work on this problem as soon as possible."

"Okay. Will you be able to work with crutches?"

"Sure, it's only a mild sprain, and I do most of my work sitting down anyway. So, it won't be a problem."

"Good, because I have an appointment with you after work, and I don't want to miss it."

"Not to worry. How's your shoulder feeling now?"

"It doesn't seem to be getting any better. I'm getting a sharp pain in my shoulder almost every time I try to use it. I hope I won't need surgery because I can't afford to be out of work for weeks just to recoup."

"It has only been two weeks since we started your therapy. So, let's not talk about surgery just yet. Are you still doing the exercises every day?"

"Every day, just like you showed me."

"Okay, let's give the exercises another week to work."

"Okay, but I like that lotion you gave me. It really helps with the pain, but it's just about gone. Could you possibly give me more of it?" Bette asked.

"Okay. I'm glad the lotion gave you some relief. I'll have the tech give you more when you come in today. Just remind me, so I don't forget."

"Don't worry. I won't let you forget. The pain is my constant reminder that I really need the lotion. It keeps the pain tolerable, and it enables me to keep going. Thanks, Drew. I'll see you later."

CHAPTER 9

Jasmine decides it is time to talk to the mob about her suspicions. At five foot three and weighing 110 pounds, she is glamorous wearing a powder blue body-hugging wool skirt suit, silk blouse, matching high heels, and a Louis Vuitton purse. She goes to the smallest of the two restaurants in the upscale hotel. Pauli and Anthony Saffarino are sitting in the red leather booth located at the back of the empty restaurant. They can be found there most days in the closed restaurant's dim light taking care of business. Standing behind them are two giant bodyguards. Both are as big as 300-pound football linemen with faces that look like they stayed in the fight business too long. The bulge under their left arms screams concealed weapons.

"Good morning, gentlemen," Jasmine said. "You know, with all the years I have known you, I still can't tell you two apart."

The identical twins are delighted since they always enjoy confusing people by dressing alike. First, they kept their light brown hair short. One parted his hair on the right while the other one parted his on the left. Then after a few months, they would change their part again to cause more confusion.

Each of them wore a tailored black double-breasted suit with a snow-white shirt and a maroon silk scarf tied around their necks. They looked like a mirror image of each other.

And they never corrected someone if they guessed the wrong name.

"Good, that's how we like it," Pauli said. "How can we help you today? Have the hotel rooms been okay?"

"Oh, yes. The rooms you've provided for me have been perfect," Jasmine said. "But that isn't why I'm here today. I have a different problem. I have a bad feeling about one of my regulars."

"What do you mean?" the twins said simultaneously.

"He's been asking to see me, but he doesn't have any money."

"Do you want us to talk with him?"

"No, I can handle him. He's just annoying," Jasmine said as she tapped her long, perfectly polished red nails on the table as she told them her story.

The Saffarinos' agreement with Jasmine was to provide her with nice hotel rooms to entertain clients, a separate private suite for herself, and protection if needed. In return, she takes care of the twin's sexual needs and any mob lieutenant that may come down from New York. She also gives the brothers 10 percent of her earnings.

"John 22 has been seeing me for a couple of years, and something just doesn't seem right with him."

"Like what?"

"Well, he claims to be from Cleveland, but he doesn't know anything about the area. He keeps telling me how wonderful New York is and how he wants to take me there and show me the sights. It just doesn't add up."

"What does he look like?" Anthony asks.

"Well, he's about five foot ten and weighs about 170 to 180 pounds. He is almost totally bald except for some brown hair on the sides and the back of his head. Also, he wears a gold lucky horseshoe, diamond pinky ring on his left hand. John 22 told me he bought it for himself after his wife divorced him, and he had his first big win. Also, he works at the Hands-On Physical Therapy off Hwy. 441."

"We already know the guy we're looking for works at that therapy place. We had the boys break in there a while back to see if we could find out something about him. We gave them a note to put on the wall. We're looking for a man that weighs over 300 pounds and has a full head of hair, so I don't think it's the same guy. Besides, the six guys working there are all about five foot ten, except the owner is six foot two. We'll eventually figure out which guy we're looking for," Pauli said.

"How did you know to check out the therapy place?" Jasmine asked.

"The guy we're looking for is the one that ratted out the Don about eleven years ago. He was a bookkeeper for the mob and took a lot of money," Pauli said.

"He also testified that he witnessed the Don killing a couple of guys. That put the Don on death row. Everyone knows the Don wouldn't kill anyone. He would have one of the guys do it for him. After he testified, he just left town, and we've been looking for him ever since. So, when his wife came to us and asked if she could make a deal, how could we refuse? They got a nasty divorce, and she wants to get back at him, so she tells us where her husband was working. She said she missed her family and wanted to return to her former neighborhood and start over again without her husband."

"Why didn't she give you his new name while she was telling you about him?" Jasmine asked.

"Hey, this guy was so big, he couldn't hide in a crowd. We didn't think we needed his name, but we're not doing so well figuring out which one is the right guy. Who would have thought he would lose so much weight and lose his hair? We'll talk to his wife again if we don't figure out who the right guy is soon. So, that won't be a problem. Now, if you need help with your non-paying client, we'll be happy to show him the right way to do things."

"John 22 is just a nuisance, and I can take care of him so far. I'm okay now, but I'll contact you immediately if it gets too difficult. I just wanted to talk to you both about this to ensure I'm doing the right thing. Thanks for listening to me. I appreciate all your help."

"You know we're always here to help you."

CHAPTER 10

Steele is in his small office finishing up the reports from the last two days, but, his work is interrupted when Nancy texts him to come to her office.

"Did you get the results of the background check yet?"

"Of course, I did, but you're not going to like the results."

"I figured he did this before because people are creatures of habit, and he didn't just start gambling today or embezzling money to pay for his gambling problem," Steele said as he sat on one of the uncomfortable chairs around Nancy's desk.

"No, it isn't that. Your perp has a clean record and not even a parking ticket. The part you aren't going to like is Hudson's financial history only goes back ten years. I couldn't find any record of credit cards or bank statements before that time. During the last ten years, he also got divorced, passed the physical therapy assistant state-administered national exam, and got his certification to be a therapy assistant. I don't know how he managed to pass the background check eight years ago for the certification with a limited financial and work history. He does have a Florida driver's license but no record of any other driver's license before this time in any other state. He has two maxed-out credit cards in his name. I don't know even how he got the credit cards."

"That is interesting. I'm going to have to find out more about this Hudson guy. Did you check with Interpol? Also, did you check to see if he's on social media?" Steele asked.

"No sign of him anywhere. I looked everywhere I possibly could. He doesn't have anything on Facebook, Twitter, Instagram, or LinkedIn, which is unusual. I think everyone has at least one picture with other people or something on one of those networks," Nancy said. "I looked in every possible place, and there is nothing about him."

"Everyone has a paper trail of some kind. You don't just fall off the grid."

"Well, this guy appears to have fallen off, but no one noticed," Nancy said, giving him a flirty smile.

The detective checks with the FBI because their focus is to stop terrorism, organized crime, and serious crimes such as serial murders. The next step is to go to the CIA, even though they only collect data outside the US. The only place left is to contact the US Department of Justice, looking for any information about Will Hudson. But no one has any knowledge of him, and Steele is obsessed with finding out more about Hudson and wondering why it's bothering him so much. Hudson is just another case, but he doesn't like unanswered questions. There is something about Hudson that Steele just can't figure out.

Steele muttered, "There has to be an explanation for all of this," as he reminded himself to stop his habit of mumbling.

He heads over to the therapy shop again to get Will Hudson's fingerprints.

"Hi, Mr. Spencer. Do you have a minute?"

"Sure, come into my office."

"I need to get fingerprints from Hudson and hope you can help me."

"Sure, what do you need?"

"Anything that he recently touched would be beneficial."

"He left his coffee cup here this morning. So, you can have that if it will help."

"That would be great. I'll get this back to you as soon as I can. Don't tell Hudson why I have his cup."

"You can count on me, Detective."

Lt. Steele holds the cup with his thumb and forefinger, careful not to disturb any fingerprints, and puts the cup in an evidence bag. Then, he takes the cup to the lab and asks them to run the prints to see if they find any useable ones.

CHAPTER 11

Bette is outside her unit enjoying a smoke before cleaning the shop for the end of the day when Pete joins her. They begin to talk.

"Why don't you let me cut your long hair? You would look much better if I cut off that scraggly ponytail."

"I kind of like my scraggly ponytail, if you don't mind."

"Well, at least let me wash your hair. You would look a lot better."

Ever since he met her after starting work as the pizza delivery guy, Pete has had a crush on Bette. He enjoys meeting her in the alleyway to smoke and talk. Although almost twenty years younger than her, he hopes he will get the courage to ask her out. Also, having Bette touch his hair while cutting it would be pretty enjoyable. But if she cuts his hair, Pete fears she won't notice him anymore, and he couldn't tolerate that. But when Bette suggests that she could shampoo his hair and make it look better. He is delighted with her suggestion and agrees. Pete enjoys the closeness of Bette shampooing his long hair and blowing it dry.

"Now, your hair looks a lot better. Let's go back outside to finish our smoke break."

Will shows up as they are just finishing their cigarettes. He sees a black alley cat coming toward him and kicks the cat away.

"Now, why did you do that? That cat wasn't bothering you," Bette said.

"I'm superstitious, and I don't like cats, especially black ones. So, if a black cat crosses my path, I kick them out of my way," he said with a sneer.

"I didn't realize that you were such a mean person. But while you're here, do you have a minute? I need to talk to you. Come inside."

"What do you want, Bette? You're not going to start bugging me about the loan, are you?" Will said as they walked to her office.

"No, I just have some news for you."

"What kind of news would you have for me?"

"I just wanted to tell you that I'm pregnant."

"What? Didn't you use protection? Are you going to get rid of it?"

"Of course, I'm not going to get rid of our baby. I thought you would be happy. I know I'm keeping the baby. So why didn't you use protection if you didn't want to have a family? We are both responsible for making this baby," Bette said.

"You expect me to be happy. How do I even know if it is mine? It could be Pete's. He's always hanging around you. Or it could be anyone's, and how sure are you that you're even pregnant?" Will shouted.

"I used a pregnancy test from the drugstore yesterday, and it was positive. I only see you, and you know that. There isn't anyone else."

"Well, don't expect me to support the kid. You should just get an abortion," Will said as he stormed out of her office.

Bette was bewildered. She thought Will would be as happy with their baby as she is. Bette never thought he wouldn't want to start a family after telling her he loved her so many times. Confused she doesn't know what to do. She does know that getting an abortion is out of the question. Bette could never kill her baby.

Pete comes in the back door and finds Bette in her office sobbing. He sits next to her on the couch and puts an arm around her. Holding Bette is something Pete has dreamed about for a long time. He didn't want it to be under these circumstances, but he is still happy to be holding her.

"Hey, Bette, is everything okay? How can I help you?" he asks as he rubs her shoulders.

"I just don't know what to do. I thought Will would be happy that I was pregnant, but he didn't want anything to do with the baby. In fact he said I should get an abortion."

"I didn't know you were pregnant."

"I just found out myself yesterday."

"Don't worry about that now. Just relax, and we'll figure out what to do. Together we'll come up with a plan that will be the best thing for you and the baby," Pete said.

"Thanks, Pete. I appreciate you helping me. But you can't tell anyone about the baby for a little while until I figure out what I'm going to do. I don't want everyone talking about my problems behind my back. Okay?"

"Sure, Bette, whatever you want. Your wish is my command. You know I would do anything for you."

"Thanks, Pete. I know you're a special guy."

CHAPTER 12

Lt. Steele goes to the Investigations Department and walks over to Nancy's desk after lunch.

"What is the big rush? Your text message said to get over here ASAP. What's going on?"

"There is a US Marshal in your office, and he is fuming. Just thought you should know before heading in there," Nancy said.

"Thanks, I appreciate the warning."

He heads to his office, expecting the worst. *What does a marshal want with me?* he wondered on the way to his office. The marshal is sitting in Steele's tall back chair behind the large, steel desk cluttered with dirty coffee cups, unfinished reports, and an old computer.

The room has three filing cabinets, each with three overstuffed drawers, a wastebasket overflowing its contents, and two visitor chairs. The walls are painted Army green making the room appear small and dismal even with the room's small window.

"What can I do for you?" Steele asks as he walks into his office.

The wiry man stands up to his full five foot seven stature and holds out his small, feminine hand to shake Steele's big paw. Steele's large hand engulfs the extended hand, and he wonders how this little guy ever became a US Marshal.

"My name is Agent Robert Nice with the US Marshal's office from the US Department of Justice," he said proudly. "When you put the fingerprints of one of our witnesses in the computer, red flags alerted us that you were checking on him. I want to know why you're running the fingerprints of one of the guys under our protection? You don't have any right to check on him."

"I'm trying to find out why William Hudson doesn't have any background for more than ten years. Is that your witness? Then, I want to know all about him and what he was doing before that."

"I cannot confirm or deny that he is one of our witnesses. Is this person you're checking on in some kind of trouble?" Nice asked.

"It seems like he's embezzling funds from his employer to pay off gambling debts, and I just want to know if he has done this in the past?"

"Everyone in the Witness Protection Program and everything about them is confidential. The records are sealed. So just back off and leave him alone. I want you to stop checking on him, and I don't want to come back here again. Do you understand?" he growled as he left the room.

"Just keep your witness in line, and I won't have to keep an eye on him," Steele mumbles to the retreating figure.

Feeling discouraged and intrigued by the visit from the marshal, Steele wants to find out more about Hudson. However, his phone rings, disturbing his thinking. Nancy tells him they found a stiff off of Seven Mile Drive in the alleyway a few minutes ago.

"Okay, I'm on the way. Is Wagner heading that way too?"

"Knowing Jack, he'll be there before you even get to your car," she said.

At least this isn't an early Monday morning call, and Steele wasn't jolted out of a sound sleep. He's mumbling to himself as he heads to the scene and reminds himself to stop this habit of mumbling. The traffic is heavy with all the working people, snowbirds, and tourists clogging up the roadways. He finally arrives and wonders how the coroner's van is already there when the road is so backed up with traffic. CSI Jack Wagner is busy collecting evidence from the body. He also notices the reporter is already at the scene.

"What are you doing here?" Steele asks Parker.

"You know I work for the *Village Chronicle*, and I heard about the dead body on my police scanner and came right over."

"Well, if you have to be here, just stay out of my way," he tells her. Turning his back to Parker and addressing Wagner, Steele asks, "What do you have for me? I hope it won't take long. This humidity is killing me," he added as he wiped his forehead with a handkerchief.

"It has been extremely hot for September. Did you ever try putting a wet cloth around your neck to help with the heat?" Wagner asks.

"No, thanks. I'm already wet enough."

The sweat makes it difficult for Steele to put on his disposable gloves.

"Well, he looks like a gang member, but I don't think it's one of ours. He has a large python tattoo on his right forearm going up to his neck with the snake's head peeking out from the top of his T-shirt. He also has a few small prison tattoos on his body, but the snake is a professional job and the most outstanding one. He doesn't have any gunshots or knife wounds, and it doesn't appear anyone strangled him," Wagner explains. "Also, there isn't any evidence of blunt force trauma."

"So, you have no idea what killed him?"

"It looks like a robbery gone wrong, and as you can see, his jeans and jacket are fairly clean. Not like someone that was in a fight. You'll have to wait until the coroner gets him on the table to find out what killed him. But I can tell you from his liver temp that he has been dead for at least eight hours.

"Just let me get a pic of the snake so I can check it out on the gang database before you put him in the body bag."

Steele also takes pictures of the body lying face down on the ground, then turns the body over to get a picture of the victim's face. The victim has the muscular body of a bouncer and appears to be about six feet tall. He checks all the pockets, but they are empty. He doesn't have a phone, jewelry, wallet, or any identification on him.

"The perp took everything. There isn't any money or keys. The killer emptied his pockets and then turned them inside out. He didn't have any defensive wounds either," Wagner said.

"Then he must have known his killer." Steele thinks this will be a challenge as he continues to check out the body and surrounding area for any helpful clues.

"Who found him?"

"Someone was cutting through the alley and saw the dead guy next to the dumpster and called 9-1-1," Jack said.

"Jack, did you get the victim's fingerprints?"

"Of course. It was one of the first things I did when I got here. If you completed your investigation of the victim, I would let the coroner's assistant take the body."

"Sure. Go ahead. I'm going to walk around here and check out the area. The alley smells like a dump with all the dumpsters overflowing. Why hasn't the garbage been collected? How can you work with this foul smell? It doesn't look like it even bothers you," he said to Wagner.

"Here, put some of this menthol salve under your nose. The salve will mask the smell of garbage."

"Thanks for the salve. I wouldn't have thought something like this would help with this terrible nose-burning smell."

"I think one of the garbage collection companies went out of business. No one seems to be interested in getting the garbage company's clients. So, no one is cleaning this mess. Soon, people will complain, and somebody will eventually take care of it," Wagner said

After a careful search, he doesn't find anything to help him with this case, and he returns to his office.

Ashley Parker stays a bit longer and talks with Wagner to get more information. She is handling the putrid stink of garbage by holding a handkerchief doused with perfume by her nose.

After Wagner confirms her information, she is happy to get back to her office to write the big story about a murder occurring in The Villages. The crime rate for this area is so low that having a murder victim is a rarity, making this a great story.

Back at the office, Steele tries to get his computer to bring up the gang database to check out the snake on his victim. But unfortunately, he never did well with electronics, and the computer is his nemesis, which he has been trying to overcome.

He texts Nancy asking for her help. He is grateful Nancy has already taught him how to use his phone to text and take pictures. It has made his life a lot easier. She enjoys going to his office to help but snickers at his incompetence.

"It is very straightforward," Nancy said.

The database appeared on the computer screen after she typed in the correct web address for the police agency's criminal intelligence system that stores information on identifying gang members.

"Okay, tell me what you want to know."

"Look up python tattoos on the right forearms and go up the arm until the head of the snake tattoo is on the person's neck."

"Oh, that sounds awful." Then, after a few keystrokes, a picture of the dark brown, scaly python with diamond-shaped beige streaks appears on the screen.

"That's it. What does it say about it?"

"Look, you will never learn if you don't do some of this yourself," she playfully scolded him.

He would prefer if she would just get him the information, but he knows she is right. After scrolling through pages of information, he finally finds the page he wants. A description below the picture of the giant snake is the gang called the "Palatka Pythons." Palatka, Florida, is the gang's headquarters, and they are known to sell all types of drugs. They also buy and sell snakes as a sideline. An applicant must wait to get a python tattoo until after they have been considered to join the group. If the applicant doesn't fulfill all qualifications, they don't become a member. Only gang members are allowed to have the tattoo of the large python on their right arms. Any other requirements for joining are not known. According to the Palatka Police Department, the gang is considered heavily armed and dangerous. Approach with extreme caution.

Steele wonders why a Palatka gang member would be down here just to hang around? Their clubhouse is about 75 to 100 miles away, which is a long way from home. How did the victim get killed in an alleyway if they were so dangerous? What happened to his weapon if he was supposedly heavily armed? He had to know the perp because he doesn't have any defensive wounds, or they snuck up on him, but that isn't possible. The guy is really big, and he would certainly notice if someone were coming up behind him. Steele is confused about all the unanswered questions he has about this gang.

CHAPTER 13

Pete and Bette meet out back for their usual last smoke before cleaning and closing up the shop for the day. They sit on the bench recently set up against the wall between the beauty shop and the pizza place.

"How are you feeling?"

"I'm doing okay. I went to the doctor today, and he said everything looked good. He confirmed that I was pregnant, and he gave me some vitamins for the baby and me."

"Now that the doctor has confirmed your pregnancy, I think you should stop smoking. It isn't good for the baby.

"You're right, Pete, but quitting isn't easy. Nevertheless, I will do my best to stop."

"Do your best, and I will help you quit smoking. We can still come out here and talk. Also, I was thinking about us, and I want to help you with your problem about the baby."

"What can you do, Pete?"

"I have a three-bedroom house, and I thought you could move in with me until the baby comes and I can take care of both of you. Then, you would have your own bedroom, and after the baby comes, you could consider moving into my bed. Then, maybe, we could talk about getting married if you will have me. What do you think?"

Bette always enjoyed talking with Pete outback during their smoke breaks, but she never thought of him in a romantic way. He isn't a bad-looking guy with long black hair and a lean frame. It would be nice to have a man around to take care of her and the baby. He is only five foot seven, making him only a few inches taller than her. She also notices how young Pete looks. She is concerned that the age difference between them will cause a problem later.

"I don't know, Pete. Your suggestion is all so sudden. Let me give your proposal some serious thought, and I will let you know later."

"Bette, I have loved you for a long time, and I would do anything for you. Don't worry about the difference in our ages. Everything will work out. I have enough love for both of us. Would you please give this a lot of thought? This proposal is important to me," Pete said.

"I will seriously consider this, but how can you possibly afford a large house and have money to care for the baby and me? You can't be making a lot of money as a pizza delivery guy."

"Don't worry, and I have enough money to take care of us and the baby. I've been doing a lot of work on the side and getting paid under the table. Trust me. Money is not a problem for us."

They extinguish their cigarettes in the old coffee can next to the bench and return toward their businesses as Drew comes outside.

"I just came out to congratulate you on the new addition and wish you well," Drew said.

"How did you find out about it?" She turns to Pete angrily. "I told you not to tell anyone."

"Don't worry, Pete didn't say a word. It was your beauticians. They are telling anyone that will listen," Drew said.

"How did they find out?"

"They probably figured it out because you're already throwing up every day with morning sickness," Pete said. "You're also very moody, which is not like you."

"Sorry, Drew, I didn't mean to bite your head off, but I'm still adjusting to all of this myself. Did Will say anything?"

"No, why would he say anything?"

"I feel you should know. Will is the father, but now he won't even talk to me. He claims it isn't his."

"Well, that explains his unusual actions," Drew said. "He also seems to be very irritable lately, which is normal. But, of course, he's always been a negative and depressing person, so that hasn't changed. He does seem to be grumpier than usual, so I appreciate you telling me. It clarifies his terrible behavior."

CHAPTER 14

Steele thinks it is time to check out the cold cases and see if they are connected to the current murder.

He goes to the CSI office in the back of the police station to find CSI Matt Lombardo and Wagner. Their office is a lot bigger than his. Unfortunately, the room has also been painted the depressing Army green color, making their room look puny. They have two large desks against the walls filled with mountains of manila files for all the current cases they are working. There is also a long table in the middle of the room with a computer and laboratory equipment to analyze the crime scene's evidence. All fluids, blood, hair, and fingerprints go to their lab for analysis.

"Good afternoon, gentlemen. Could you help me find the info on the cold cases about the past murders in the alleyways?" Steele asked.

"We would like to help you, but there was a fire in the evidence room about six months before you transferred here. Wagner explains that the fire destroyed all the pictures and notes on our cold cases."

"So, there isn't anything for me to compare to this new murder?"

"Sorry, Grant, but there isn't anything. The only thing that stands out in my mind is they weren't from our local gangs."

"Wasn't anything saved in the computer?"

"Of course, but the info is put on a thumb drive and kept with the rest of the evidence. Sorry to tell you. The fire destroyed everything," Lombardo said.

"Who was the detective working on the past cold cases? He should remember some facts about the case."

"The lead detective retired about a year ago and then had a fatal attack," Lombardo said while looking at his computer.

"Well, can you guys help me with the computer to find information on our local gangs? I would ask Nancy, but all she does is laugh at me."

"Sure, what do you want to know?"

"Just give me everything on the local gangs here."

"We don't have gangs here, just a couple groups of teens trying to stay out of trouble. So, the local police started a proactive program for the kids in the neighborhoods around The Villages. They stay in touch with them regularly to stay ahead of any potential problems," Wagner said.

After a few seconds on the computer, Wagner gives Steele a page from the printer with all the local gangs' information.

The printout showed three groups in the local area. They are all docile and don't cause any trouble for the police. The first one was the Dragon Lords. The small group of teenagers spends their time racing their sport bikes in the large Walmart parking lot after the store is closed. They are all good kids and don't bother anyone. A small fire-spewing, yellow dragon tattooed on their left forearms can identify them. The yellow dragon represents noble companions, which is why the teens picked this specific color. Their group motto is for everyone to take care of each other and work diligently to keep everyone out of trouble.

The next club is the Book Worms. A group of teens helps their contemporaries learn how to read or help tutor them if they fail in their schoolwork. The group is designed to help the teens and their friends to reach their ultimate goal of having everyone graduate from high school. They have at least two adults guiding and overseeing them to help achieve their goals successfully. This program has been helping troubled kids graduate from high school for years. The group is identified with a squiggly green worm holding a small book stenciled on their shirts. The kids aren't allowed to have any kind of tattoos, smoke, or swear, and the adults enforce this rule for the kids to stay in the program.

The third is a gang of older boys called the Privileged. This clique wears a navy-blue blazer with the circular crest of two swords crossing over a world on their left breast pockets. The colleagues all live in a large house with five bedrooms and two and one-half bathrooms in a quiet residential neighborhood outside The Villages. The group acts more like a college fraternity than a local gang. They have a miniature gold crown tattooed on their left inside wrist. A watchband can almost cover the crown, making it difficult to identify them without their blazers. Still, every member must come from a wealthy family and have unlimited available funds for their use.

According to the local police departments, all the kids in the gangs are good. None of them have criminal records, and they don't cause any trouble.

CHAPTER 15

In desperation Bette calls Will at the office and begs him to come to the beauty salon so they can talk.

"Please, Will. We need to talk. It's important."

"Okay, but this better be worth my time. I'll be there at lunchtime when no one is there."

After her last customer for the morning, Will comes in the back door and meets Bette in her office.

"There is nothing to talk about unless you want to get an abortion, then I'll pay for that."

"Now, Will, I already told you that is not going to happen. I won't kill this baby. It is part of you and me."

"Well, you need to stop telling everyone that I'm the father of your child."

"I want you to take a paternity test so I can prove to you that you and only you could be the father."

"No, that's not going to happen. I'm not giving you or anyone else my DNA. I just want you to leave me alone. Is that clear?"

"Did you already forget about all the money you owe me? You had better figure out how you plan to pay me because I want my money back. I will need it to take care of the baby."

"Well, I don't think that's going to happen. You don't have any proof that I borrowed any money from you. I didn't sign a note agreeing to pay you back. So, you can forget about getting any money from me," he said loudly with his arms outstretched.

Will slams the back door as he leaves. Bette starts crying. Pete is outside smoking and sees Will leaving in a huff. Pete enters the beauty shop and sits next to Bette on the couch. He puts his arm around her shoulders and rubs her back until she stops crying.

"What did he say this time?"

"He won't take a paternity test, and he says he won't pay back the $3,500 he borrowed from me. I didn't get him to sign any papers when I gave him the money saying that he would pay me back. I should have known better than to trust him, because this happened to me in the past. I lent money to a family member a couple of years ago, and they never paid me back either."

"Okay, but there has to be some way we can get Will to pay back the money," Pete said.

"I don't know how because now I don't have any legal recourse to get my money back. I should have had Will sign a paper stating that he owes me the money. Now I don't know what to do. I need that money because I don't know how much longer I'll be able to work. This pregnancy is already causing my ankles to swell after being on my feet all day."

"Did you give him the money in cash or a check?"

"I gave him the first $500 in cash, but the $3,000 I gave him with a check since I didn't have that kind of cash on hand."

"Do you get the canceled checks back from the bank every month?"

"Of course, I get the checks back. I keep them to prove what I pay out in qualified expenses every year for my taxes."

"Find the check you gave him and put loan on the memo line. I don't know if it will be legal proof for you or not, but at least you can try. It is your word against Will's anyway."

"Thanks, Pete. It sounds like it just might work, and I'm going to give it a try. I guess I will have to go to small claims court if I want to get my money back anyway."

"I will be with you the whole time. And remember I told you that I would take care of you and the baby. So, with me at your side, money is not a problem for you. You shouldn't worry your pretty little head about this," Pete said lovingly.

CHAPTER 16

Steele sends Nancy a text inviting her to dinner Tuesday evening. She responds that he can pick her up at the office after work at 5:00 p.m.

Just before quitting time, she quickly goes to the bathroom and changes from her uniform into a summer casual dress and lets her long, naturally curly brown hair hang loosely down her back.

"You look lovely this evening. And your perfume is very nice too."

"Thank you, Grant. That is very sweet of you to say. You also look very handsome in your sport coat. Where are we going to dinner?"

"Well, I thought we could go to the Olive Garden since I owe you a nice meal, if that is okay with you?"

"That sounds great, but I don't remember if they put tablecloths on their tables. But any place would be an improvement over the Roach Coach's hot dog stand."

"That's right, and I did say I would take you to a nice restaurant with tablecloths. Are you sure the Olive Garden be okay?"

"Yes, that will be fine. Did you make reservations?"

"No, I called, and they said that we wouldn't have a problem getting a table. The restaurant doesn't take reservations, and it is still early, so we should be okay."

After being seated, they order dinner and a glass of wine. Grant and Nancy enjoy great conversation while eating the warm garlic bread sticks and salad before Steele's phone rings.

"Oh no, not tonight." He licks the garlic salt and butter dripping off his fingers before answering his phone. The dispatcher tells him there is a Signal 7 on Long Key Drive just behind the stores.

"Have to go. There's another dead body just a couple of miles from the last one. I'll make this up to you. Can you get a ride home?" he asked her as he leaves money on the table for the dinners that hadn't yet arrived.

"Sure, I won't have any problem getting home. Don't worry about me. I'll enjoy my dinner just fine without you," she said, giving him a sweet, suggestive smile.

Steele leaves to fight rush-hour traffic with snowbirds and tourists clogging up the roadway. He wishes he had a blue light on his unmarked vehicle so he could just go around the slow-moving traffic at times like this. But instead, the uniforms use marked units, and the investigators have to use the unmarked police cars that don't have any blue lights installed.

He is hungry and disappointed that he didn't spend the evening with Nancy. Finally arriving at the scene, he sees that CSI Wagner is already busy checking out the body and taking a lot of pictures. The coroner's van enters the alleyway and pulls around Steele's car.

"Do you have an extra pair of gloves? Unfortunately, I forgot to restock my supply," Steele asked Wagner.

"You can get some gloves from the case in the back seat of my car."

As Steele puts on the disposable gloves, he notices the reporter arriving.

"I can't believe that reporter is here again."

Turning his attention to the body, he asked Wagner, "So, what do you have for me?"

"This body looks just like the last one. The only difference is somebody killed the guy early this morning. His liver temp makes it about twelve hours ago, meaning someone killed him about 5:00 a.m. to 9:00 a.m. We have the same tattoo of the python on his arm and neck. There isn't any ID in his pockets, and he doesn't have any money, keys, or a phone on him. There are no obvious signs of how someone killed him, so you'll have to wait for the coroner to tell you. Also, there are no defensive wounds. It doesn't look like he fought with his killer either. There is no evidence of blunt force trauma. Otherwise, the two murders look about the same."

"What did I miss?" Parker asked as she joined the group.

"I can't believe you're here again. What do I have to do to get rid of you?"

"You can't get rid of me. This is my job," she said.

"Who found him?" Steele asked, turning back to Wagner.

"Another anonymous call to 9-1-1 saying there is a body out here but nothing else to identify the caller."

"The tattoo looks like the same inker did the job on both of the bodies. I want to take some pictures to compare them."

"Let me know when you've completed your investigation so the Medical Examiner's assistant can bag and tag the body and take him to the morgue."

"Just let me take a few more pictures, and I'll be finished. This guy looks about six foot two. Do you agree?"

"Yeah, he does look a bit bigger than the last one. The coroner will give you all that info after he gets him on the table."

"How long will it be before the coroner can start the autopsy?" Steele asked the ME's assistant.

"He should be able to start on it first thing in the morning as long as we don't get any more bodies. Right now, we don't have a backlog," Dick Morgan answers while putting the body in the bag for transport.

Steele is disappointed that the investigation has taken so long. It's too late to join Nancy at dinner. She's probably finished eating and gone home by now.

The reporter asked Wagner more questions before leaving the scene.

"Don't let Steele get to you. He's really a nice guy, but he is a bit rough around the edges," Wagner explains. "You'll get used to his manner in time."

"Thanks, I appreciate that," she said as she left to write another big news story.

Her shocking news story is above the fold on the front page of the next day's paper. The headline and story report that a second murder has taken place in the normally quiet and crime-free Villages. The residents are getting worried about a possible serial killer in the area. The police do not have any suspects at this time. According to the police department, the two victims appear to be from the Palatka Python gang, and the manner of death has not yet been determined. If anyone has any information about the murders, they are to contact the police.

CHAPTER 17

Starting a new day, Steele stops by the medical examiner's office hoping to find answers.

"Hi, Doc. Do you have some results for me on the latest murders?"

"You're in luck, Detective. I just finished the second autopsy, and they appear to be almost identical."

"What do you mean by that?"

"After I got the bodies open, their insides looked almost the same. The first one is six feet tall and weighs 210 pounds, and has a deformed forefinger on his left hand. The second one is six foot two and weighs 240 pounds. I would say they are both in their twenties. They both have severe lung damage and inflammation of the nose's membrane, which has caused a hole in their nasal septum. In addition, there is significant heart damage, and it appears their heroin addiction has caused significantly smaller brain volume. I would assume all this was the result of snorting heroin for a long period of time, possibly years."

"Snorting heroin didn't cause their death, did it, Doc?"

"No. Of course not. The two bodies we have here were murdered with a poison that someone injected into their buttocks. I found the obvious injection site while looking for the cause of death. When I get the tox screen back, I'll tell you exactly what killed them."

"Well, that is a strange place to get a deadly dose of anything," Steele mumbles.

"A female probably administered the injection since they are usually smaller than men, and the murder weapon of choice for women is often poison. The angle of the shot goes from the bottom of their butts upward."

"Thanks, Doc. That is very interesting. Call me when you get the results. I also want to talk to you about some cold case murders from a couple of years ago. Do you remember anything from the autopsies of the cold cases with murders in the alleyways?"

"Unfortunately, I was on sick leave during that time. I had a heart attack, and it kept me out of work when those murders took place, so I didn't do any of the autopsies on the victims and don't have any information for you."

With this new information, Steele visits the CSI lab. He needed to talk this over with someone to figure out what is happening.

"Hi, Lombardo. Is Wagner here?"

"No, he's at the new police diversity training today."

"What's that all about?"

"With all the problems in the country, the police commissioner decided we need to update our training again."

"Didn't we have the training when I first transferred here?" Steele asked.

"We did, but the chief says we need a refresher course. So, we all have to pay because a few people haven't learned and are still causing problems."

"So, a few people screw up, and we all have to have diversity training again?" Steele said.

"Apparently, attending the class does not change how some people think or do their job. So, everyone will attend another session, hoping to learn how to reduce prejudice and discrimination. The program is scheduled for everyone over the next eight months. You'll get your turn too. Fortunately, I'll be retired before they can schedule me," Lombardo said.

"When are you going to retire?"

"I already put my papers in, and my retirement begins in two weeks. So, after twenty years, I'm counting down the days until I leave, and I can't wait to start retirement and stop working."

"Good luck to you," Steele said as he headed down to Investigations to see Nancy.

"Did you have any trouble getting home last night?"

"No. After I had enjoyed a wonderful dinner, I called Uber for my ride home. I hope you don't mind, but I took your dinner home in a doggy bag for tonight."

"Good, I'm glad it didn't go to waste."

"How was your signal 7?"

"That's why I came down here to discuss this case. None of it makes sense. An injection in the perps' butts murdered these two big guys. There isn't anything to identify them except for the huge python snake on their right arms. I know they're part of the Palatka Python's gang, but that's it."

"Why don't you talk to Lombardo or Wagner? They could help you more than I can."

"Wagner is at a diversity training, and Lombardo is just counting the minutes until he retires."

"I didn't know Lombardo put in his papers."

"Yeah, he retires in two weeks, and he claims he's looking forward to retirement."

"Well, good luck to him. He certainly put in his time. I thought you guys already had diversity training."

"He said we have to have the training again because a few bad apples didn't learn from the first session."

After Steele leaves, a reporter for the *Chronicle* stops by Nancy's office for information on the murders.

"Hi. I'm Ashley Parker with the *Village Chronicle*, and I would like some info on the recent murders," she said, handing Nancy her business card.

"It's nice to meet you, but where is the older gentleman that used to come in for the police reports?" Nancy asked.

"He retired, and I've been promoted to take over the police beat in addition to doing features and the news."

"Well, congratulations on your promotion."

"I'm excited to learn about police procedures. I was at the scene of the murder last night and curious if there is any additional information."

"Good. So, let me tell you about the protocol to get information. Lt. Grant Steele is the lead investigator on this case, and he will have a press release at the front desk as soon as he has information to share with newspapers. You can also look over the accident and incident reports from the previous day to see if you have anything for another story. So, you can check daily, if you like."

"Thank you for your help. I'll check every day," Ashley said.

CHAPTER 18

Vicky arrives at work looking very professional in her emerald green pant suit complimenting her green eyes, her shoulder-length red hair is pulled back in a bun. Drew explains her presence to the employees.

"Vicky is here because we need help with the books. It seems there is a glitch with Medicare and the insurance billings. Vicky is going to find and fix any problems she discovers."

Everyone accepts the explanation except Hudson. "We are also having a financial problem. So, I want to ask all of you to be understanding while things get worked out. I'm sorry to tell you that I won't be able to make this month's payroll, and I hope you'll be patient with me."

Since the beginning, the employees have been with Drew and are loyal to him. They are surprised by this news because they have plenty of business since six orthopedics doctors refer patients to them for their physical therapy needs.

"We appreciate that you have a problem and hope we can help you in any way," physical therapist Chuck Vaughn said. They have been friends for years, and when Drew started his business, Chuck joined him. "It will be tough, but I'm sure we can all manage without this month's paycheck," Chuck said.

"I'll do my best to make this up to all of you. I'm grateful to have such a great bunch of guys working here. When everything gets straightened out, I'll tell you all about it," Drew explains.

Vicky settles into a routine of fixing the books on the computer. She quickly finds errors showing Will skimming funds from the business. One item reveals $8,000 was listed for security cameras, but they were never installed. She works diligently putting the books back in order and shows Drew how they can get back to paying their bills.

"Drew, the books show he used the money for the cameras five years ago," she explained in the privacy of his office.

"I can't believe Will was stealing from us all these years and still acted like he was our friend."

While talking, the computer signals a message.

"Look, Drew, a fifteen-year reunion of your Physical Therapy graduation has been scheduled. This is wonderful news. The reunion is scheduled for this weekend, and the wives are invited. Can we go?"

"I'm not in the mood to party right now, and we don't have the money. I'm still not feeling well," he said.

"Honey, we can put this trip on our credit card, and by the time the bill comes in, we'll have the money to pay it. We need to have some fun and forget about all the problems for a while. Besides, it's been a while since we had a romantic weekend together in Orlando. Also, you might be able to relax and feel better without any stress for a while."

"Okay. You win, and this could be fun. But you have to make all the arrangements?"

"I have two days to get everything done. It won't be a problem."

Vicky manages to make the arrangements and goes home to pack their suitcases. On the day to go to the hotel, she tells Drew to finish with his last patient since it's time to leave.

Arriving at the hotel, Drew and Vicky meet Larry Bellamy while they all sign in at registration table.

"Hi, Larry, I can't believe it's been fifteen years since we graduated. It's good to see you. I would like you to meet my wife, Vicky."

"Drew, it is good to see you and meet your wife. I've meant to call you for some time to apologize."

"Why would you apologize to me?" Drew asks.

"You were right about Alice. I should have listened to you."

"What are you two talking about?" Vicky asked.

Larry explains that Drew took Alice away from me while they were in school.

"When she returned to me, we married and moved to Chicago right after graduation. Drew tried to tell me that Alice was high maintenance and not right for me. I thought she was a sweet girl, but I was wrong. I should have listened to him because she had several affairs before she divorced me. It was a good thing we didn't have any kids."

"I can't believe you took Larry's girl away from him, Drew. You were always the nice guy," Vicky said with a bit of a laugh.

They head to the hospitality room to continue talking and enjoy refreshments. The room has a large banner welcoming the 2006 class. Trays of sandwiches, fruits, and a large crystal bowl of punch are available for the guests. Each fill their plate with food and retreat to a corner table.

"How are you doing?" Larry asked before he took a bite of his ham sandwich.

"Right now, things aren't good. I have a nice business with another physical therapist, two assistants, and two rehab techs. One of the assistants is a co-owner with me, but he's been stealing money from the business for years. Right now, I'm fighting foreclosure on my building."

"Gee, that is terrible. How are you dealing with everything?"

"He's not doing well financially or physically. That's why I forced him to come to the reunion, so he could relax and forget about his troubles for a little while," Vicky explained.

"You do look tired. Are you okay?"

"Just a little run-down, and I have horrible night sweats. It's probably just stress."

"Well, I hope you feel better, but I'm glad you decided to attend the reunion because I could use some help too," Larry said. "I left my job in Chicago after the divorce and thought I would look for a position down here when I got the reunion invite. So, I was hoping you could help me find a job."

"I would like to help you, Larry, but I'm tied up right now. I can't do anything until I get rid of the foreclosure problem. Can we stay in touch until things clear up at the office?"

"Sure, I have enough money saved to take a little vacation here in Florida. I also heard a lot about the famous Florida mouse, which will allow me to visit him. I'll give you my phone number, and you can call when you get things straightened out."

"Okay. That sounds like a great plan," Drew said.

CHAPTER 19

On Friday afternoon, Bette discovers all her money is missing from the cash box in her desk drawer. Then she calls 9-1-1 and tells them she was robbed, but the robber is gone. Bette has a sign at the front door which explains her cash-only policy. She doesn't take checks, credit cards, or debit cards. Bette doesn't want to pay the extra fees to the credit card companies, and she doesn't want to get stuck with a bounced check. So, Bette always takes the money to the bank every Saturday afternoon before lunch, and this plan has worked for years until today.

Lt. Steele arrives at the beauty shop just after Wagner pulls into the parking space in front of the door. The two of them walk into the shop while putting on their disposable gloves.

"My name is Detective Grant Steele, and this is CSI Jack Wagner. You reported a robbery?"

"I'm Bette Thompson, and I own this shop. I just discovered about $1,500 was taken from my cash box in my desk drawer. I won't know the exact amount until I add up my receipts."

"Why do you keep so much cash in the shop?" Steele asked.

"It has been a very hectic week, and I only take cash. I always take the money to the bank every Saturday afternoon before lunch. Any additional funds that I make that afternoon I keep until the next week."

Wagner dusts the cash box and the desk drawer with fingerprint powder, looking for any prints the perp may have left. He is also checking both doors for damage.

"There doesn't appear to be any signs of forced entry, Lieutenant. All the fingerprints were wiped clean, and I can't find any good ones."

"Thanks, Jack. Miss Thompson, do you lock your doors?"

"No, Detective. I keep the front door open for my customers, and the back door is unlocked so I can take smoke breaks throughout the day. I lock everything when I go home."

"So, someone could come in the front door and take the money while you are outback on a smoke break."

"I guess you're right. I didn't think of that before."

"Well, it wasn't a robbery because there wasn't a threat against you, and it wasn't a burglary because someone didn't break into your shop. So, what we have here is theft. A lot of people get those two words confused."

"Thank you, Detective. I learned something new today."

"Do you have any idea who would take your money?" Steele asked.

"No, everyone here is my friend. I don't have any idea who could have taken it."

"How many people know where you keep your cash?"

"That would be Drew and Will from the therapy shop and Pete from the pizza parlor next door. Also, some of my customers would see where I keep the cash when I've had to make change for them. I've never had a problem in all the years I've been here. I can't think of anyone that would rob me."

"Okay, Miss Thompson. Here is my card, call me if you think of anything else. We'll write up the report, and you can get a copy in a couple of days for your insurance company claim," Steele said.

After the men leave, the reporter enters the beauty shop and talks to Bette.

"Hi, I'm Ashley Parker from the *Village Chronicle*. I heard on the police scanner that you reported a robbery. Could you tell me what happened here?"

"Well, like I told the detective, someone stole about $1,500 from my cash box. I never take credit cards or checks because I don't want to pay the extra fees for credit cards, and checks can bounce," Bette explains.

"Did the detective say how the robber got in here?" Ashley asked.

"The detective said it wasn't a robbery. It was a theft. He said they probably walked in while I was out back having a smoke."

"Do you have any idea who might need money enough to rob you? Is there anyone that hangs around here that doesn't belong here?"

"No, this is a safe area."

"Thank you for your time, Miss Thompson," Ashley said as she left with the information for her story.

Bette goes out back for a smoke and sits next to Pete.

"Pete, I just had a horrible thought. What if it was Will that took my money?"

"That could be a possibility. Will is always broke or trying to get everyone to lend him money. Why did you think of him?"

"That reporter asked me if I had any ideas who might need the money enough to rob me? Of course, my first thought was Will. What do you think?"

"You know, you just might be right. Did you tell the detective?"

"No, I just thought about it. Do you think I should tell him?"

"Let's talk to Drew and see what he says," Pete said.

"Hi, Drew, do you have a minute? We would like to talk to you about something important."

"Sure, come into the office. What is this all about?"

Bette and Pete explain their theory about Bette's robbery and how Will is always broke and asking everyone to lend him money. Then they ask Drew for his opinion on what they should do.

"I agree with you that Will is a good suspect for the robbery, but before you talk to the detective, do you have any proof that Will did this?"

"No, of course, we don't have any proof."

"Well, why don't you find a different place to hide your cash and don't tell anyone where you put it. But let's not make any accusations until we have proof," Drew said. "We don't want to get into any kind of trouble."

"Okay, thanks, Drew. I appreciate you being here for me. I know I can count on you to help me," Bette said.

CHAPTER 20

"Hi, Doc. Your message said you have the result of the tox screen," Steele said.

"It took a while, but I finally have some answers for you."

"Okay. Don't keep me in suspense any longer. Tell me. What killed them?"

"The two bodies were killed with a drug called Carfentanil."

"Is this something new?" Steele asked.

"It is a powerful animal tranquilizer. It's sold under the trade name of Wildnil as a general anesthetic for large animals and it works quickly. It's extremely potent, which makes it inappropriate for humans. They both had enough in their systems to kill the proverbial African elephant. They also had a lot of heroin in their systems. Enough to show they were both addicted to heroin."

"I've never heard of Carfentanil," Steele said.

"It's a drug 10,000 times more powerful than morphine making it very deadly. In addition, it's currently the most toxic synthetic opioid known."

"Where could you possibly find Carfentanil?"

"Nowadays, you can find anything you want on the internet, especially on the dark web."

"Is this a legal drug?"

"Only if you're a veterinarian and using it to tranquilize large animals. This drug, like anything else, can be found on the internet. If you're determined, you can find anything."

"I'll have to check and see if I can locate it," Steele said. "But I don't do well with the computer."

"I've only come across this drug a few times during my career, but recently, I had five guys in here who overdosed on heroin and Carfentanil."

"I didn't hear about that. So, they were murdered?"

"No, I listed the cause of death as an accidental overdose. Somebody probably mixed it in with the heroin and, being inexperienced with drugs, and they didn't know it was a deadly combination. They all worked for Mr. Dempsey of the Dempsey Dumpster Company and appeared to be experimenting with the drugs. None of them had any signs of addiction that I could find. So, I figured they were trying drugs for the first time to get high and just didn't know what they were doing and overdosed."

"Thanks for the info, Doc," Steele said.

Trying to find answers, Steele visits Dempsey Dumpsters and talks to Mr. Dempsey.

"I'm Lt. Grant Steele with FDLE. Could I ask you some questions about your employees that recently died?"

"I don't know what I can possibly tell you. I couldn't ask for better employees."

"Did they have any problems, like gambling? Did you notice if they were using drugs?" Steele asked.

"To the best of my knowledge, I don't think any of them were into gambling. They never showed any signs of drug use, and I require periodic drug tests from all my employees. They always passed the drug test. All five have been with me for years and always showed up on time. They never gave me any trouble. Unfortunately, when they all died in a few days, I didn't have anyone to run their routes. The garbage piled up, and I lost my customers. I didn't have any choice, so I had to file for bankruptcy."

"Did they have personal problems that you knew about?"

"No, they became good friends. Joe was going to get married in a few weeks, and the rest of them were in his wedding party. As I said, they worked together for years and became good friends. All five of them have been with me for several years, and they were good employees. They have always been model workers and were a happy-go-lucky bunch of guys. It is going to be difficult to replace them. I don't know what happened to them or what possessed them to try drugs. None of this makes any sense. It was out of character for them," Mr. Dempsey said.

The men continue their discussion and do not notice the young woman entering the office.

"Hi, I'm Ashley Parker from the *Village Chronicle*," she said. "Hello, Detective, and you must be Mr. Dempsey. I would like to ask you some questions about your employees."

"What are you doing here?" Steele asked.

"Mr. Dempsey's employees were recently killed with the same drug that killed the two men in the alleyways, and I want to ask him some questions."

"How did you find out about that?"

"The medical examiner was nice enough to tell me when I asked him."

"I don't want that information about the Carfentanil in the news just yet because it will interfere with my investigation. So, just for a while, can you put a hold on this?"

"Sure, if you give me an exclusive when you solve this case."

"That won't be a problem. So, do I have your word?" asked Steele.

"Of course, it will be nice working with you, Detective."

After getting information from Steele, Ashley writes an updated news story about the Alleyway Murders. She gives details about the murders and their victims. She is careful not to mention the Carfentanil drug in the story because she wants to get the exclusive story promised to her by Detective Steele when the murders are solved. Getting the scoop on this story would greatly help her career. She gave her word to the detective, and she was brought up to understand that your word was your bond. She believed that giving your word is sacred, and she always kept her word.

CHAPTER 21

Bette walks into the therapy clinic Friday morning holding her shoulder while wincing in pain.

"Hey, Drew, I'm in a lot of pain. The pain is stabbing and sharp, and it doesn't seem to be getting any better. Can you help me?"

"Sure, Bette. I'm busy right now. Can you come back later? I could fit you in after lunch."

"What should I do until then?"

"Call your doctor and tell him about your increased pain. Then put some ice on your shoulder. Twenty minutes on and twenty minutes off. That should help until I can see you."

"I'll try the ice. Thanks, see you later," Bette said.

Bette returns to the therapy clinic after lunch, still in severe pain.

"Tried the ice, and it helped a bit. But I couldn't reach the doctor, so I had to leave a message."

"I'll do an evaluation to see if you made any improvement since you started with us. Did you do anything to reinjure your shoulder?"

"No, I've been very careful not to reinjure it, but it just seems to be slowly getting worse. I'm starting to get a sharp pain in my shoulder when I try to move."

"Okay. Let's take some measurements, and we can try different kinds of exercises and stretches. Before you leave, I will rub more of the No Pain Freeze lotion on your shoulder, which will help."

Drew takes measurements and continues to record the movements of Bette's shoulder to compare to the measurements from two weeks ago.

"I'll send the results of your new measurements to your doctor and explain your increase in pain. I'm sure his office will call to make an appointment and discuss the next step in fixing your shoulder. I will have Allen fix you another jar of the No Pain Freeze to take home. That will help with the pain until you can reach your doctor."

"I'll get right on it, Boss," Allen said.

"I'm not busy right now, and I can fix the jar for you," Will said after his patient left.

Will goes to the counter pulling on disposable gloves to prepare the concoction and gives the jar to Bette.

"Thanks, Will," Bette said.

Drew rubs the lotion on her shoulder, giving her some relief.

"Thanks, Drew. I appreciate all the help you have given me."

"I'm just sorry we couldn't fix your shoulder for you."

"That's okay. I know you tried," Bette said before going to her shop to take care of her last client for the day.

"Are you all right? You're as white as a sheet, and you're shaking," Bette asked her lady.

"Did you see those goons outside in that car? They backed their car into the parking space next to mine and are just looking out their front window at the building," her client said as she entered the shop.

"What are you talking about?"

"Just look out the window. Do you see the guys in the car?"

"They do look like a couple of hoodlums. Did they say anything to you?"

"No, they just glared at me when I parked. The thugs just scared me. Why don't you call the police?"

"I will. The hoodlums don't look like they belong here."

It didn't take long before the local police car appeared. The cop gets out of his car and talks to the men. After a few minutes, the mysterious car leaves the parking lot. Then the officer enters the beauty shop and tells Bette and her client.

"Don't worry, ladies. They said they were waiting for someone. And I told them to wait in a different place. I don't think they'll be coming back. But if they do, just give us another call."

"Thanks, officer, for getting rid of them. They were scaring my client."

"Not a problem. We are here to protect and get rid of scary people for you."

"Thanks again. I appreciate all you do for us."

74

Now that the police have taken care of the problem, the ladies continue talking about the creepy guys and wondering why they would be in the parking lot. The ladies continue to speculate while Bette shampoos and styles her client's hair.

With all the excitement of the thugs outside, Bette doesn't notice her pain, and she leaves the jar of pain relief lotion on her desk when she goes home for the day.

CHAPTER 22

Steele decides to try a local hamburger joint for lunch. He is enjoying a giant hamburger and french fries with a super-sized soda. Just as he shoved the last greasy fry in his mouth, he noticed a big guy with a python tattoo going up his right forearm with the snake's head on his neck enter the fast-food joint.

This is too good to be true, he thinks to himself. *Today must be my lucky day,* he thinks as the stranger orders food and takes his tray to a table.

Steele took his trash to the container. He walked back to the tattooed guy, showed his badge, and said, "My name is Detective Grant Steele with the FDLE. May I sit down?"

"I ain't done nothin' wrong, so you can just go and leave me alone so I can eat my food."

"Oh, I thought you might want to know where your gang members are."

"What do you know about them?"

"If you want, I can take you to them," Steele said.

"Just tell me where they are, and I'll find them myself."

"They've been murdered and are in the morgue. Do you want to see your guys or not?"

"No, just tell me what happened."

"How about you tell me your name and the names of your buddies?" Steele asked.

"I don't have to tell you nothin'."

"If you want to know what happened to your guys, you will answer my questions. Now, just give me the names," Steele asked with authority.

"You don't have to be so pushy. I'll tell you. I'm The Boss, and my boys are Snoop and Buster," he said.

"What are their last names and addresses?"

"We don't have last names because when you join our gang, you get a name for the job you're gonna do. We live together in a deserted barn just outside of Palatka. No one lived there for a long time, and we just took it over."

"What are you and your gang members doing here?"

"I'm not telling you nothin' else," the Boss said.

"Don't worry. You won't get into trouble if you haven't done anything. I already know that your gang is involved in drugs. Is that why you're here?"

"No, I haven't done anything wrong. I just got here today."

"That's good. Now tell me the reason your boys traveled here?"

"Snoop came here to snoop out the area to see if he could find a new group of people and sell them some drugs. We heard The Villages were building up, and they had a lot of older people here. So, we thought this would be a good place to set up our business. When he didn't come back, Buster came out to bust some heads if needed to help Snoop. So now I'm here to find out what happened to both of them."

"Did they have drugs with them when they came here?"

"Sure. You can't sell drugs if you don't have them," the Boss said.

"Well, when we found them, they didn't have drugs, phones, ID, or anything else."

"They both wore a heavy gold chain with a gold snake pendant hanging off the end of the chain, just like mine. I want the necklaces back when you find them because only the Pythons can wear these. We had them made special for our boys. They also carried Taurus 9mm semiautomatic guns, and I want them back too."

"You will get necklaces back when we find them, but there is no way you're getting the guns back. Could your guys have just used all the drugs themselves?"

"No, they took enough drugs to sell for a while and still have enough for themselves."

"What kind of drugs did your boys try to sell?"

"We only deal with horse."

"Only heroin? Are you sure?" Steele asked.

"Sure, I know what my boys are doing."

"Have you or your boys ever used Carfentanil?"

"Hey, I don't know what you're talking about. Like I said, we only deal with horse, nothin' else."

"Do you sell pure heroin?"

"No way, you can't make any money selling dope without cutting it with a lot of corn starch. Besides, pure horse is too strong for the everyday druggie."

"I'll let you go without any problems if you promise to stay away from this area with your drug dealers. Then, when we find the killer of your guys, I'll let you know."

"Sure, not a problem. I'll go back and work on getting my boys home," the Boss said as he left the restaurant.

"That will be good. But remember to stay home and don't come back, or I'll put you in jail for dealing," Steele said, talking to the Boss's back as he walked away.

Steele will have to check in with pawnshops to see if he can find the gold chains or the guns. Now he has another clue to finding information.

CHAPTER 23

After having a lengthy debate with himself, Dick Morgan, the medical assistant, decides to talk with the detective. They meet at the neighborhood coffee shop for a cup of joe and sit at a table in the back for privacy.

"Thanks for agreeing to meet with me, Lieutenant," Morgan said as the young waitress served the coffee.

"Are you ready to order or do you need another minute?"

"No thanks. We'll just have coffee today."

"What seems to be concerning you?" Steele asked Dick after the coffee was served.

"When the tox screen came back with Carfentanil in it. I knew I had to talk to you."

"What could you possibly know about this drug?"

"Besides being the ME's assistant, I'm also a PI in my spare time, and I met with the first guy murdered."

"Why did you become a private investigator?"

"I couldn't make it on my state salary, so I needed a second job to make extra money. My young son has cancer, and I have so many medical bills I'll never get out of the red. So, I had to do something to make more money. I also thought it would be interesting to become a private investigator."

"I'm sorry to hear that about your son. Now tell me what's going on. And what do you mean you met with the dead guy?"

"My client hired me several weeks ago to check on possible drug traffickers coming into town. My client said he wanted to make sure the area stayed safe. I contacted the first drug dealer on the dark web, so I didn't recognize him at first in the morgue. He wore a hoodie that hid his tattoo and most of his face when we met. It wasn't until later that I remembered he had a deformed forefinger on his left hand. When I saw his hand in the morgue a couple of days ago, I remembered our meeting."

"Okay, now you can tell me about your meeting."

"I contacted him on the dark web and told him I wanted to make a large purchase."

"How did you get on the dark web?"

"Getting on the dark web isn't a problem. All I had to do was download a dark web browser. After I installed the browser, it was easy."

"Okay, how did he react to your request?"

"He wanted to meet right away. He then told me how he was cutting the heroin with the Carfentanil. He said this drug was less expensive and easier to get on the internet than actual heroin. It only takes a tiny amount of Carfentanil mixed with just a smaller dose of heroin to get high. That way, he can make a lot more money."

"Did he say if the gang always works this way?"

"No, he became agitated when I mentioned his gang. It looks like he wanted to make extra money for himself by selling the altered heroin, but he did tell me he sold some of the altered drugs to a bunch of guys having a bachelor party. He said it was Joe's last chance of freedom before getting hitched."

"Well, that explains how the Dempsey Dumpster workers were killed. Now tell me what you did with the drugs that you bought?" Steele asked.

"Of course, I didn't buy any drugs. That's illegal, and I didn't want to lose my license. When I met the drug dealer, I told him that I only wanted pure heroin because I knew he wouldn't sell me the pure stuff. After all, he couldn't make any money selling it that way. He makes his money by cutting the heroin and having more product to sell."

"So, who is your client?"

"You know the client is confidential, and I'm not under obligation to reveal their identity."

"Can you at least tell me if any more drug dealers come into town?"

"Sure, Lieutenant. That is something I can do using the dark web."

Now Steele has another piece of the puzzle, but it still doesn't help him solve the murders. He still needs a lot more details.

CHAPTER 24

Vicky arrives at work alone on Monday and tells the guys that Drew isn't feeling well. He won't be in until later because he's at the doctor's office.

"As you all know, Drew has been taking chemo for his T-cell LGL Leukemia for fifteen years. The doctor gave him stronger chemo two months ago because the original medicine stopped working. After two months, the new medication was doing its job, but Drew started having night sweats. We think Drew had side effects from the stronger medicine, so he went to the doctor to get some answers."

"Don't worry, Vicky, we can cover all the clients coming in until Drew gets here," Chuck Vaughn said to comfort her. "I'm sure everything will be all right. Don't worry."

The day goes smoothly until Drew calls to tell Vicky that Dr. Martin, his cancer doctor, has ordered an MRI of his chest and he will be at the office after that.

Later in the day, Dr. Martin calls Drew and tells him he is scheduled for a PET scan the next afternoon because the MRI showed he has stage-4 lung cancer.

Drew is overwhelmed as he tells Vicky the horrible news. Vicky and Drew talk about how the cancer diagnosis will affect them. They stay up all night praying for help, consoling each other, and talking about what to do. After the PET scan, they go to the doctor's office for the results.

"The PET scan shows a large mass in the upper right lobe of your lung. The mass appears to be stage-4 lung cancer, but you need to have a lung biopsy to determine what kind of cancer you have," Dr. Martin explains. "If you have small-cell lung cancer, you will go quickly, but you should have five years tops if you have non-small cell lung cancer."

Vicky starts to cry. Drew is in shock as he listens to his doctor giving him the information to see Dr. Jacobson, a doctor specializing in radiology, to do the biopsy. Dr. Martin has managed to get an appointment for the lung biopsy for the Wednesday afternoon.

"Do you want me to call you and tell you the bad news after I get the biopsy report, or do you want to come into the office later for the outcome?" Dr. Martin asked.

Trembling, Vicky tells the doctor, "I want you to call us immediately and give us the results."

"Well, I don't want you to say I gave you bad news over the phone," Dr. Martin said.

Visibly upset, Drew and Vicky leave the doctor's office and head home to prepare to see the specialist the following afternoon. Finally, after a sleepless night, they drag themselves out of the house and head to the doctor's office for the biopsy.

"It has been a rough couple of days. Why don't we stop for a cup of tea before we go for the biopsy? We have plenty of time, and a cup of tea might make us both feel better," Drew suggests to his wife as they were on the way to the specialist.

"If you think we have enough time, that would be a great idea. That would be enjoyable, and we can put off the inevitable for a little longer."

They stop at a restaurant just a few miles away from the radiologist's office and enjoy a cup of tea and some quiet time together, discussing their bleak future.

They finally decided they had better get to Dr. Jacobson's office and have the procedure.

Drew is prepped for the biopsy while Vicky anxiously paces in the small waiting room. Finally, when the nurse motions her that she can see Drew, she goes to the procedure room with her heart pounding and sees the imaging specialist with a smile on his face.

"I couldn't do the biopsy because there was a big abscess, and I drained 40 ccs of gunk out of his lung," he said. "I put in a drain to get rid of the rest of the abscess, and we will start him on antibiotics tomorrow. It appears the lung abscess showed up on all the scans, and the doctor assumed it was stage-4 lung cancer. So, the good news is that it doesn't look like Drew has lung cancer, but we have to put him on strong antibiotics daily for several weeks to get rid of the rest of the abscess. Come back tomorrow morning, and I will put in a PICC line in thirty minutes. It will make it easier to get the daily infusion of antibiotics at the clinic."

"Oh, thank God. Our prayers have been answered. I feel so relieved with this wonderful news. Thank you, Doctor."

With their burden lifted, they happily head for home.

"After I get the PICC line installed tomorrow, I'm going back to work," Drew tells his wife. "I want things to get back to normal as quickly as possible."

"Are you sure? Maybe you should spend a few days at home first to rest."

"No, I'm ready to go to work. As soon as the doctor took that stuff out of my lung, I felt great. Now that I'm feeling better, I don't want to waste any more time. I still have to go for a daily infusion of antibiotics, but I can do that during lunchtime. I'm behind in a lot of work, and this will give me a chance to catch up. Besides, the guys have already done so much for me. I don't want to impose on them any more than I already have."

"Okay, you're the boss, but you know the guys would do anything for you," she said.

CHAPTER 25

Bette has been trying to stop smoking because of the baby. Pete also asked her to quit, but she isn't doing well fighting off the cravings. Finally, Bette gives in to her urges and goes out to have her usual cigarette break before closing the shop and heading home. After stepping outside, she sees two men standing over a man on the ground and starts screaming. Her screams bring Pete running from his unit to comfort her.

"Are you okay? You look like you've seen a ghost, and your shaking like a leaf," he asked as he puts his arms around her and sits her down on the bench.

All she can do is point at the man on the ground. Pete dials 9-1-1 to tell them there is a dead body in the alley as the two men run away.

It doesn't take long for an ambulance, squad cars, and Lt. Steele to pull up in the alley. The blaring sirens bring Drew into the alleyway.

Lt. Steele is heading to the body when he sees the paramedics putting the man on the gurney.

"What do we have?" the detective asked the paramedic.

"We have a middle-aged white man that someone has severely beaten. He may have some broken bones in his face, and we know he has a compound fracture of his right arm. His breathing is shallow, and his blood pressure is low. He's in shock but still alive. Unfortunately, you will have to wait to talk to him at the hospital."

The medics put the stretcher in the ambulance and headed to the hospital with sirens blaring and lights flashing.

"Do you happen to know who the man was?" Steele asked Drew.

"Sure, that was Chuck Vaughn. He's my friend and has worked with me since the beginning. This beating has to be a random attack."

"Have you seen anyone hanging around here lately?" the detective asked.

"No, it's usually quiet out here. I don't know any reason why anyone would beat up Chuck," Drew said.

"Wait," Bette speaks out. "I'm Bette Thompson, and I met you when you took the report on my robbery. Oh, I forgot. I meant the theft."

"Yes, Ms. Thompson, I remember."

"We had a couple of thugs here a few days ago. They were sitting in a car in front of the building. It was scaring my customer, so I called the police. The officer talked to them, and they left."

"Thanks, Ms. Thompson. Can you tell me what you saw tonight?"

"Sure. There were two white guys. They looked like those big goons in the car outside my shop the other day. Both were wearing black suits with white shirts. It looked like they were kicking a body on the ground. They ran when I screamed. It's a good thing Drew finally installed some lights out here because I saw the two guys as soon as I stepped outside."

"Thanks, I'll check it out. Do you think you would be able to recognize them?"

"No, I know I won't be able to recognize them. The men were so ugly. That's all I remember. It all happened so fast."

"Here is my card if you think of anything else," Steele said.

Steele checks with Dispatch to find the officer that talked to the men in the parking lot a few days ago and asks him to come to the scene. It only took five minutes for the uniform to arrive at the scene since he was already working the night shift.

"I talked to the guys, and they left. They said they were waiting for someone, but they didn't give me a name," the officer reported.

"Did you get a license number, or can you at least give me a description of the men?"

"Sorry, LT. They backed in, so I didn't see the plate. The two guys were massive like football players, but they were sitting in a black Cadillac Escalade, so I don't know how tall they were."

"Okay, but if you think of anything else, let me know," Steele said as he dismissed the officer and headed to the hospital.

A young man on a bicycle rides up to Steele as the uniform officer leaves.

"I saw the guys get into a car," the teenager tells him excitedly.

"What did you see?"

"I saw two big white guys jump into a Black Escalade, and they drove north on Hwy. 441 just as I was entering the alleyway.

"What are you doing in the alley?"

"I was going to be late getting home, so I took a shortcut. My mother would kill me if I was late again."

"Did you get a good look at the guys?"

"No, they were just big, but I got the license plate if that helps," he said enthusiastically.

"Wonderful. What did you see?"

"It was a Florida plate with a horse on it and the letters HJN."

"Good job. Thanks for your help. Now get home before your mother comes looking for you."

Steele heads to the hospital, and it doesn't take him long to find a nurse with information about Chuck.

"What can you tell me about Chuck Vaughn?" Steele asks the nurse as he shows his badge. "He was brought in by ambulance a while ago."

"They just took him to radiology to do a CAT scan of the brain to make sure he doesn't have a brain bleed. After checking for internal bleeding, they will take him to surgery. He appears to have a ruptured spleen, a broken cheekbone, bruised kidneys, and his fractured arm also has to be set. He also lost a lot of blood. His injuries are consistent with someone repeatedly kicking him. The man was badly beaten and is lucky to be alive."

"When will I be able to talk to him?" he asks.

"It will be a least a couple of hours before he is out of surgery and the anesthesia wears off."

"Thanks, I'll be back later. Here is my card. Will you please call me when Mr. Vaughn is awake?"

"Sure, Detective."

As he leaves the hospital, he sees Drew and Vicky.

"Hi, Lieutenant. We thought we would check on Chuck before heading home."

"The nurse said Chuck would be in surgery soon, and he won't be able to have visitors until tomorrow," Steele said.

"Thanks. I guess we'll just go home and see Chuck in the morning. Please keep us informed if you find the people that did this."

"Of course. By the way, did you get your security cameras installed?"

"No. Will just took the money instead of putting in new cameras," Vicky explains.

"We should have installed the cameras as soon as we discovered the old ones weren't working, but we just didn't have the money to do the job," Drew said.

"That's okay. We'll still find the guys that did this."

CHAPTER 26

"I can't believe everything that has happened in the last few days, and now Chuck is beaten. It just seems like we can't get over this streak of bad luck that we're having, and it's starting to affect our friends too," Drew tells Vicky.

"I know, but I'm sure there is a logical explanation for all of this," Vicky tries to be encouraging since she is not superstitious. "It has to be a case of mistaken identity. Chuck doesn't have any enemies. He's a good guy, and everybody loves him."

"Chuck will be out of commission for a while. So, how will I handle all of our patients by myself?"

"Why don't you call Larry Bellamy and see if he can help out until Chuck can return?"

"At least now that I'm working on the bookkeeping, instead of Will, we're back to making money again," Vicky said. "You can offer Larry a good salary if he's still interested in working with you."

"That's a good idea. I'll call Larry tomorrow. I hope he'll be ready to go to work."

"Since we can't see Chuck until tomorrow, why don't you text Larry and see if he can meet us for lunch? Then, maybe he will be ready to start work."

Larry answers the text to say he would be happy to get together. So, they agreed to meet for lunch the next day.

Looking good, six foot tall Larry Bellamy enters the restaurant wearing gray slacks, a navy-blue blazer, light blue dress shirt with a red and black Garcia tie.

"Hey, buddy, you don't look well today. Are you doing okay?" Bellamy asks Drew.

"It turns out that we aren't doing very well at all."

"Why? What happened?"

"My physical therapist Chuck Vaughn was beaten up in the alley yesterday. He is in pretty bad shape and won't be able to work for some time. We were hoping you would be ready to start working with us."

"I'm sorry, Drew, but I won't be able to start right now. It seems my funds didn't go as far as I had hoped. I didn't realize the Disney World attractions and living in Orlando would be so expensive. I almost ran out of money."

"So, what did you do?" Vicky asked.

"I didn't have a choice. I had to get a job and start working at Dillard's Department store. I was able to purchase some clothes with the employee discount. Fortunately, I can talk to people, and I am good at helping choose the right clothes for them. Which is great since I work on commission."

"Is that why you look so handsome today?" Vicky asks.

"Well, thank you, ma'am."

"Drew, why can't you look that good too? You always wear jeans and a T-shirt. If you wore a nice pair of slacks and a dress shirt, then you would look professional when you put on your lab coat at work."

"You can come into the store, and I will fix you up with the right clothes. I can use my employee discount so we can get you a good deal."

"That sounds great. How much longer do you have to work for Dillard's?" Drew inquires.

"When I started, they gave me a small bonus, so I have to stay for another week to complete my commitment, giving us plenty of time to get you a new wardrobe."

"Okay, I can work with that. But I really need you to help with the business. Will you be able to start after that?"

"Of course, that would be perfect. I'm staying at an extended stay hotel in Orlando, which is something I can afford. Next week I will check out apartments closer to the clinic."

"Thanks, Larry. That will be great. I need your help, and I'm looking forward to working with you. If you need financial help, I can give you an advance on your first month's pay to help you."

"Thanks, Drew. I would appreciate the advance, and then I will have enough money to put a deposit down on an apartment."

CHAPTER 27

"How are you doing today?" Detective Steele asks as he walks into Chuck Vaughn's room.

"Right now, my face and body feel like it was used as a football in a rough game. Fortunately, the pain meds are working and controlling the pain. The doctor said I was lucky since the broken ribs didn't puncture my lungs."

"Good. Can you remember anything from the night someone beat you?"

"I was leaving to go home when these guys jumped me from behind as I left the building. I remember that they kept calling me Frank."

"Are you sure it was Frank that they were calling you?"

"I'm positive. I don't even know anyone named Frank."

"Is there anything else that you remember?"

"Only that someone was hitting me over and over. I didn't understand anything they were saying. Everything was all garbled. They kept screaming something in my face, and I could see that the guys were white and grotesque. So, if they were calling me Frank, they weren't after me. The guys must have me confused with someone else."

"It sure sounds like mistaken identity to me too," Steele said.

"I'm so glad that woman screamed. After that, the guys stopped kicking me and ran."

"That woman was the beautician next door."

"I'll have to thank her when I get out of here. I think she saved my life," Chuck said.

"We have two witnesses that agree with your description of your attackers. Also, one of the witnesses got a partial plate number, which will help us find the owner."

"Good, then you should be able to find them quickly."

"We will do the best we can, but we only have a partial number."

While Steele is interviewing Chuck, Ashley walks into the room.

"Hi, Mr. Vaughn. I'm Ashley Parker from the *Village Chronicle*. May I ask you some questions?"

"What are you doing here?" Steele asks her.

"I just need a little more information on Mr. Vaughn's beating. You're not going to object, are you?"

"No, of course not. Just stay out of my way."

"I know we have an agreement, but I have to work on other stories too. Now, may I talk with Mr. Vaughn?"

"We just finished, and I was just leaving. Chuck, give me a call if you think of anything else," Steele said, walking out of the room.

Ashley interviews Chuck and gets all the details of the attack for her news article. They both hit it off, and they continue talking as friends. She asks if she can visit him tomorrow just to see how he is doing. Although he is already tired he readily agrees to have the company of a bright, attractive young lady.

Steele heads back to the office in hopes of finding some answers.

"Nancy, can you check a plate number for me?"

"Sure, what do you have?"

"A Florida license with a horse on it and the letters HJN on a black Escalade. Can you get me the name of the owner?"

"This will only take a minute," she said as she put the information into the computer.

"That's strange."

"What's strange? Talk to me."

"Apparently, the computer has a glitch or something because nothing is showing for the partial plate number. Also, it's not showing anything for any of the horse country plates that are already out there."

"How can that be? I thought the license plate information is automatically put in the computer when the tag is purchased."

"I'll contact the tech support team. They should be able to fix the problem."

"That would be great, Nancy. How long will it take?"

"I'll contact them now and get you an answer," she said as she typed a message to the IT team.

Steele paces in front of Nancy's desk for a few long minutes before she tells him the results.

"Well, I have good and bad news for you. Which one do you want first?"

"Okay, get serious. I've already had a bad day, so give me the good news first."

"The good news is the computer is fixed, and there are fifteen vehicles registered with that partial plate in this area, and one of the plates was reported stolen."

"You really know how to ruin my day. Do you have information on when it was stolen?"

"According to our information, the plate was stolen from a blue Ford parked at the Cosmopolitan Hotel about a month ago."

"Thanks, I'll check it out."

Steele goes to the hotel and notices the hotel guest services representative's name tag.

"Hello, Erin. I'm Detective Grant Steele from FDLE," he said, showing his badge. "Apparently, someone removed a license plate from one of your guests' cars about a month ago. Has anyone reported that somebody took their license plate off their vehicle while staying here?"

Checking her computer, she tells him, "I'm sorry, Detective, we don't have any record of a missing tag. So, possibly, they didn't report a tag missing until after they got home."

"Okay, thank you for your time, but would you contact me if anyone should report the missing plate?" Steele said as he gave her his card.

"Of course, Detective."

CHAPTER 28

Will calls Jasmine on Wednesday to make an appointment but insists she calls him by his name and not the label she gave him when they began seeing each other. In the past he didn't always have the required fee.

"Okay, Will, but do you have the money today?"

"I have longed to hear you call me by name for such a long time. Yes, I have the money. I need to talk to you about a problem I'm having. Can you see me early tonight?"

"Come over today about 4:00 p.m. I'm at the same hotel in room 501, and we'll talk."

Will nervously walks back and forth in the office until it's time to meet Jasmine. He wonders if he is doing the right thing talking to her. Arriving early, Jasmine opens the door to a nervous client, wearing a silk robe and high heeled slippers.

What is this all about? Come in and sit down. Do you want a drink?"

"Sure, give me my usual while I tell you my problem."

"Here's your drink. Now stop being so mysterious and tell me what is happening with you."

"I have a big problem with the beautician next door to my office. She said I got her pregnant."

"Did you?"

"Yes, but she was supposed to use protection. Bette Thompson is old enough to know better."

"What did you say her name was?"

"I told you, Bette Thompson. What difference does it make?"

"None at all. What are you planning to do about this?" Jasmine asks.

"I'm going to eliminate her from my life. I don't want her to be a noose around my neck with that baby. She'll want me to pay child support until it's eighteen, and I'm not doing that."

"And how are you going to manage that?"

"I already put some liquid nicotine in the pain-relief lotion she is getting from therapy to ease the pain from her shoulder. She will rub it on and die. The skin easily absorbs the nicotine, but I was careful and used disposable gloves when I filled the jar."

"Where did you get the nicotine?"

"Simple, I used the e-juice for my e-cigarette. You can get it at any smoke shop. I usually get a 15 ml bottle of e-juice, but this time I got the 30 ml bottle so I would have enough to do the job. Of course, everyone will think Bette had a heart attack and died. No problem."

"What made you think of nicotine?"

"I researched it on the internet, and too much nicotine can kill you. Besides, everyone knows she smokes, so she already has nicotine in her system."

"Do you think this will work?"

"I hope so. I gave Bette the altered lotion Friday. But she's still okay. She came in again today and asked Drew for more pain relief. She wasn't looking well, so I put in even more nicotine this time. It should definitely work tonight."

"Okay, Will, you are scaring me. Talking about murdering that lady just isn't right. There has to be another option."

"There isn't any other option. I've given this a lot of thought. She is a nag, and I want her and that baby out of my life. Killing her is the only way out."

"Do you realize that you are talking about killing a human being, Will? You're talking about murdering someone like it's something you do every day."

"Do you have a better idea on how to get rid of this woman?"

"No, I don't, but there has to be another way without killing her."

"I told you the plan is already in action, and it can't be stopped now, even if I wanted it to."

"You're really scaring me, Will. So, maybe it's time for you to leave. Or do I have to call security?" she asks, standing and holding the door for him.

Will slowly moves toward the door.

"Please let me stay, Jasmine, it's still early, and I need you."

"I'm sorry, Will. You better just leave."

Will hangs his head and slowly shuffles out the door.

CHAPTER 29

Bette goes to the clinic before lunch on Wednesday to get much-needed pain relief.

"I'm sorry to bother you, Drew, but I'm really in a lot of pain today. Can you do anything to help me?"

"Have you talked to your doctor yet?" Drew asks.

"No, I haven't. I can't even get an appointment with the doctor for another three weeks. He is so busy that he doesn't have an opening until then."

"Bette, I'm sorry. I'll call the doctor's office later and see if we can get you in sooner. But unfortunately, with Chuck in the hospital, I don't have any free time right now."

"How is Chuck doing?"

"He's out of ICU now, and the doctors are confident that he will make a full recovery. Maybe you should try doing different exercises on the full-body machine to help loosen your shoulder," Drew said.

"Okay, I'll try, but could you put some of that pain-relieving lotion on my shoulder when I'm finished? I need some relief from this stabbing pain. I'm not feeling well, and this pain only makes me feel worse."

"I'm busy right now, but Rick could do it. He's a great assistant."

"Right now, I don't care who does it. I just need some help," she said in pain.

"Rick set Miss Thompson on the upper body machine for five minutes. After that, put some ice on her shoulder for another five minutes, then rub some No Freeze Pain lotion on her shoulder."

"Sure, Boss, I can do that," he said.

"Allen, could you prepare some of the lotion for her to take home?" Drew asks.

"I can do it. I'm not busy right now. So, I'll take of it," Will said as he was pulling on disposable gloves to fix the jar of the pain relief treatment.

"Here, Bette. The lotion will help with your problems," Will said as he handed her the jar.

"Thanks, Will. That was nice of you," Bette said.

"Let me know tomorrow if you are still in a lot of pain," Drew said.

"Thanks, Drew. I'll let you know as soon as I get to work, I'm coming in late on Thursday, but I'll see you as soon as I get here," Bette said relieved.

With the pain subsiding, Bette returns to the salon to work on her scheduled clients. She manages to see most of her customers before the severe pain returns. Finally, Bette decides the pain is too much and calls her last client to cancel the appointment.

She sits on her sofa and puts more of the altered No Pain Freeze lotion on her shoulder. As the pain relief takes over, Bette lays back and enjoys the freedom from pain. She then stumbles to the bathroom and has an episode of vomiting. While severely shaking, Bette struggles back to the couch to lie down. She has waves of nausea and severe sweating but is too exhausted to go out for her usual after-work smoke.

Before passing out, she hears the jingle of the brass sleigh bells on the leather strap hanging on the front doorknob doing their job of announcing a visitor. She wonders who is in the shop, but is too sick to get up and find out.

CHAPTER 30

Last week US Marshal Robert Nice and Will Hudson entered the out-of-town diner together for their quarterly meeting. The restaurant is located twenty miles away from the busy city and is the only place they found to have a confidential and private discussion. The diner is old and in need of significant repairs. Their shoes stick to the dirty floor as they walk to a table in the back of the room for privacy. Hudson knows he is in trouble with the marshal and nervously tears apart sugar packets as they wait for their coffee.

The tired waitress wearing a dirty apron looks at the sugary mess with disapproval as she pours the coffee.

"Are you ready to order? Today's special is country fried steak with mashed potatoes and gravy with a side salad."

"If you're buying, I could use some food, and the steak sounds great," Will said.

"No, we're just going to have coffee today. Thank you," Nice said to the waitress.

"Are you really considering eating here?"

"Sure, as long as you are buying."

"That isn't going to happen. Just tell me, how are you doing since the last time we talked three months ago?" Nice asked.

"Everything is the same, but I could use more money."

"You always need more money, and you know there isn't any more money. You got a lot of money and a nice setup when entering the Witness Protection Program. So now, all we're required to do is check on you periodically. Besides, if you're so desperate to get money, why don't you sell that pinky ring?"

"This ring is my good luck, and I can't sell it, or I will sell my luck. Couldn't you just loan me some money?"

"That is not going to happen. I talked to Detective Grant Steele about you recently, and he is not very happy with you either."

"Why is he sticking his nose in my business anyway?"

"He claims you're stealing money from your boss."

"No, I'm not. All I'm doing is borrowing a few bucks, and I plan to pay it all back someday."

"You need to behave and stop borrowing money from your boss. If he decides to press charges, you'll be in big trouble, and you might get kicked out of the program. Besides, the prosecutor in New York is not happy that we gave you a walk on the self-defense shooting of your neighbor before you went into the program. He feels he didn't need your testimony to get the Don on murder charges. They were working on another angle to prosecute him and didn't need you."

"It was self-defense. My neighbor was coming after me with a hammer. So, I didn't have any choice but to shoot him. It was self-defense."

"Your ex-wife is talking to the police about you having a grudge with the neighbor. She tells them that you put the hammer next to him after you shot him. She claimed to be a witness to the killing and said it wasn't self-defense."

"Do you know what it's like knowing your ex-wife is having an affair with your neighbor? I probably should have shot my ex-wife instead of her lover, and then I wouldn't be having all these problems now. But instead, she has been nothing but trouble for me since she got the divorce. I just wish she would keep her nose out of my business."

"You should be careful not to repeat that story where someone can hear you. You can still be charged for murder, you know. There isn't a statute of limitations on murder."

"No one is going to believe my ex-wife about this. Everyone knows she is a liar."

"I'm just telling you, Will, you need to behave yourself, or they could remove you from the program. You are causing me a lot of trouble. Can't you just behave?"

"I'm doing the best I can. But it's been a while since I've been in a game, and it's stressing me out. I need money for a buy-in, and if you can't get me more money, I wish you would just leave me alone."

"I'm concerned about the way you're talking. Besides, giving you more money is there anything else I can do to help?"

"As I said, I just need to get in a game. If you can't help me with that, then there is nothing you can do for me."

CHAPTER 31

"Lt. Steele, your vehicle was broken into in the parking lot," a uniform officer told him as he was leaving his office for lunch. "Somebody broke your vehicle's passenger window, and there is glass all over the passenger seat. Did you leave anything of value in your car?"

Steele always parks his unmarked unit in the back parking lot of the police station. He enjoys the convenience of having his car close to the building. Unfortunately, the cameras don't cover the area where he parks.

"Did anyone see who did this?"

"No, LT. A uniform noticed the broken window when he walked past your car."

"Where is a cop when you need one?" Steele asks no one in particular.

He heads to Nancy's office to tell her about his recent problem.

"Hi, Nancy, do you have a minute?"

"Sure, Grant, what do you need?"

"It seems someone stole my iPad from my vehicle. All my notes, pictures, and diagrams are on the iPad. Can you get me another one?"

"I can't believe you left valuables in your car where someone could steal them. But sorry, we don't have any extra ones that you can use."

"What am I going to do? I need my computer," Steele said.

"You're a detective. Why don't you see if you can find the person that stole yours?" she said, stifling a laugh.

"Just what I need now is a comedian. Are you going to help me or not?"

"I'm sorry, but there just aren't any extra iPads available. So, I guess you'll have to resort to the dinosaur age and use paper and pencil until you get it back."

He turns and stomps back to his office.

A few hours later, a teenager wearing dirty and ripped clothes brings in the iPad and asks if there is a reward for finding the computer and bringing it to the police station?

"How did you know it belonged here?" Nancy asks the youth.

"Because it has a big police badge sticker on it, and I brought it here," the boy said.

"Why didn't you just sell it?" Nancy asked.

"I would've, but I couldn't get it opened."

"Thank you for bringing this in. Where did you find it?"

"It was in the dumpster down the street. So, when I couldn't open it, I brought it here."

"You did the right thing, and I appreciate your honesty. I'm sorry, but there isn't a reward."

After the disappointed boy slowly leaves, Nancy texts Grant to come to her office. She has a surprise for him.

The detective quickly gets to Nancy's office and sees his iPad on her desk.

"How did you find it so quick?" Grant asks.

"Oh, it was some great detective work on my part."

"Okay, let me have it. I have work to do."

"Sorry, but I have to check to make sure somebody didn't install any malware. It shouldn't take long. Then you can have it back."

"You're just tormenting me. Let me know when I can get it."

"First, you have to give me the password so I can check it out. Then you'll be the first to know.

Steele never learned touch typing, so he slowly used two fingers to accomplish the task.

"It would have been a lot easier if you just told me what it was."

"Can you hurry this up because I have a lot of work to do, and I can't do anything without my iPad," Steele pleads.

"Now go back to your office so I can take care of this," Nancy tells him.

Nancy does a quick search of the computer and discovers a suspicious file. She takes the iPad to the chief. "Do you have a minute, Chief? I have a problem," Nancy said in a concerned voice.

"Sure, Nancy, come in. What can I help you with?"

"I was working on Lt. Steele's iPad, and I found a file describing some disturbing information. So, I decided I had to bring it to you."

"What exactly did you discover?"

"A report stated that Lt. Steele almost beat a guy to death. It also shows that he needs anger management counseling."

"That report is confidential, and you shouldn't have read it."

"I'm sorry, but I was checking for any viruses he may have on his computer. Now, I'm concerned about Steele."

"There isn't any reason for you to be concerned. Steele was working undercover to break up a pedophile ring. He caught some guy in the act of molesting a child, and he just lost it and started to beat up the perp. Someone stopped him before he killed the guy. Steele is also going to anger counseling here. He will be okay. Just keep this information to yourself."

"Is this why he transferred here from Los Angeles?"

"Yes, he wanted to go to a place that didn't know about his anger problem concerning pedophiles. Just make sure you'll be able to keep this to yourself."

"Yes, sir, that won't be a problem."

"Good. Now get back to work."

Nancy takes the computer to Steele's office.

"I'm returning your stolen computer. Fortunately, no one installed a virus, and I didn't find any malicious software on your computer. So, everything is good."

"Thanks, Nancy. I appreciate your help with all this computer stuff."

"I'm always willing to help you with your computer problems."

CHAPTER 32

On Wednesday evening, a petite figure dressed in black slacks with a black hoodie jacket enters the beauty salon, jerks the noisy brass sleigh bells from the doorknob, and throws them on the floor. Walking through the shop, the intruder locks the back door before discovering Bette on the couch, either asleep or passed out. The person shakes Bette and slaps her face trying to wake her. The slap wakes Bette. Startled, she tries to sit up on the couch.

"Jasmine. What are you doing here?"

"I thought it was time for payback."

"Why are you talking nonsense? How did you find me?"

"Never mind how I found you. I now have a really sweet setup. It just proves that I didn't need you after all. I was able to survive without your help."

"Oh, Jasmine, it is so good to see you again. I'm sorry about the past. Can you forgive me?" Bette gasps.

Jasmine remembers about ten years ago when Bette was a madam in a brothel in Texas, and she was one of her girls. Jasmine had fallen in love with Taylor Dalton, a wealthy gentleman that wanted to marry her and take her away. When Bette found out about the love interest, she didn't want to lose her youngest and most desired girl. So, she told the gentleman that Jasmine had left town with another man.

Dalton stopped going to the brothel, and Jasmine did not know about Bette's betrayal until a year later when the other girls told her about it. When she wasn't able to find Taylor, she never forgave Bette. Finally, when the police started to look into the ages of her girls, Bette closed down the brothel.

She took all the money and left town, leaving the girls to fend for themselves.

"No, I can never forgive you for what you did to me. But I understand that Will has already poisoned you, so this should be easy," Jasmine said as she put the large pillow over Bette's face. Unfortunately for Bette, the nicotine was already taking effect. She was having trouble breathing. Jasmine held the pillow tight against Bette's face until she stopped struggling and went limp.

She fluffed the pillow as she heard knocking on the back door. She quickly left the shop through the front door.

"Drew, can we check on Bette?" Pete asked as he ran into the clinic.

"Why do we have to check on her?"

"I banged on her door, but she isn't answering, and her door is locked. You know she doesn't lock her door until she leaves. It's almost 6:30 p.m., and she always has a cigarette before closing the shop, and her car is still here. She's not answering her phone, and I'm worried. This isn't like her. Can you use your key so we can check on her?"

"Okay, Pete, settle down. I'm sure I have them in my desk somewhere. Okay, let's try this bunch of keys. I'm sure it's one of these."

They both go to the beauty shop's back door, and Pete loudly knocks again as Drew tries each of the many keys on the ring. Finally, after many attempts, Drew unlocks the door. They both enter, calling her name.

Pete reaches the office and sees Bette on the couch, and he kneels next to her and holds her hand. Drew is close behind.

"Bette, please wake up. Drew, call 9-1-1 and get an ambulance."

"Okay, Pete, they're on the way. Take it easy."

"Can't you help her, Drew?"

"It's okay, Pete. The rescue squad will be here in a minute."

The ambulance arrives with the police. The paramedics check on their patient and ask Pete to let go of Bette's hand and leave the room so they can do their work. Pete slowly stands up and reluctantly leaves the office.

"I want to go with her to the hospital," Pete said.

"I'm sorry, but regulations don't allow anyone but the patient in the ambulance," the paramedic tells him.

Lt. Steele arrives as the medical team is taking Bette to the ambulance.

"What is going on?" Steele asks the paramedics before going inside.

"She has already passed, and we're taking her to the morgue. She's still warm, and rigor hasn't set in yet. So, it's only been a few minutes since she died,"

110

they quietly tell Steele. "We'll leave it up to you to break the news to the boyfriend."

"No problem."

Steele enters the shop and sees Drew.

"Let's sit down for a while, and you can tell me what happened?"

Ashley Parker has slipped into the room and quietly stays in the background as she listens to Drew explain what happened.

"Pete was worried about Bette because she didn't go out for their usual smoke break at 6:30. Also, her car is still there, and the back door is locked. Bette doesn't lock that door until she is ready to leave."

"Where did you find her?"

"She was right here on the couch. She appeared to be sleeping. Earlier today, she was in my clinic, and I gave her some more pain-relieving lotion to help with her shoulder pain," Drew said.

"How long has she been using the pain-relieving lotion?"

"It's been a few weeks since she came to me for therapy. She told me the pain was severe, and I put this lotion on to give her relief," Drew said.

Pete is on the couch, holding his head in his hands and sobbing quietly.

"The paramedics told me she was already dead, and they were taking her to the morgue. They will do an autopsy on her tomorrow," the detective tells Drew quietly.

CSI Jack Wagner enters the office after checking around the building.

"There isn't any evidence of forced entry. Everything looks like it did when we were here for the burglary. If there was foul play, the perp wore gloves and wiped down the door because there aren't any fingerprints," Wagner tells Steele.

"Thanks, Jack. There isn't anything else we can do tonight," Steele said as he took the jar of lotion off the floor. "Here, take this to the lab and have it analyzed."

Steele notices Ashley standing next to the wall.

"If you want any more information, you'll have to wait for the news release," Steele tells Ashley as he leaves.

"Pete, I'm sorry to tell you, but Bette is dead," Drew tells him while comforting him.

"No, that can't be true. She was okay this afternoon. She can't be dead," Pete sobs.

CHAPTER 33

"Jasmine's Escort Service, please tell me how you got this number."

"Mac, the poker game host, gave it to me. He said to call this number for a good time."

"Okay. First, let me tell you my protocol to keep my clients unidentifiable. Everyone gets a number, and when you call for another appointment, you use the number that I give you. This way, you don't have to worry about me trying to blackmail you or give your identity to the cops if they ever raid me. Your number will be John 30."

"That'll be fine. Can I make an appointment for tonight?"

"Come to the Cosmopolitan Hotel at 8:00 p.m. I'll be waiting for you in room 501."

Promptly at 8:00 p.m., Jasmine opens the door to meet her new client. Overjoyed, she sees the tall, slender, gray-haired Taylor Dalton and puts her arms around his neck.

"I can't believe it is actually you. You are as handsome and sexy as ever. How did you find me?"

"Well, it wasn't easy. After stopping at every escort service in Texas, I headed east. I continued to visit all the escort services until I found you. After winning big at the local poker game Mac, the host, told me to call Jasmine for a good time. I knew it had to be you, but I didn't tell you when I called that it was me because I wanted to surprise you."

"Well, let's stop talking and go to bed. It has been too long."

The couple embrace. They tear off each other's clothes passionately and drop them as they fall onto the bed. The heated passion had been building since Taylor walked into the room. Then, the phone rings, disturbing their excitement.

"Jasmine's Escort Service," she said.

"This is Will, and I need to see you tonight. I can be right over."

"I have a client and can't see you right now. Why don't you call tomorrow?"

"Jasmine, this is important. You have to tell the cops I was with you all night."

"I'm sorry, Will you have to wait until tomorrow. I'm busy right now."

She hangs up the phone and explains to Taylor that Will has been stalking her for some time. Jasmine tells him how Will shows up and doesn't have any money. She also told Taylor how Will said to her that he would murder Bette Thompson, the mother of his child.

"How did you manage to find Thompson?" he asked.

"Oh, it was by accident. I had no idea Bette was here. Will told me about her. It's a long story."

"Well, just tell me the part about how this guy is going to kill Thompson."

"Will put nicotine in some kind of pain-relieving therapy lotion and gives it to Bette to kill her," Jasmine said.

"Okay, you can give me all the details later, but let's not worry about that now. Everything will be okay now that we're together again. So, let's get back to our lovemaking. We will take care of Will later," Taylor said.

Minutes later, there is a loud banging on the door. Will is shouting for her to open the door.

"Will, just go away, or I will call security."

"Please, Jasmine, open the door. I need to see you. You have to give me an alibi for tonight."

"No, just go away. I've called security."

The two security guards are looking at the boring computer images with heavy-lidded eyes. They are staring at the many computer screens showing different parts of the hotel. Then, the action of a man banging on room 501 has them jumping out of their chairs. They tell Erin, the hotel guest services representative, to call 9-1-1 as they head to the elevators.

The banging continues for a while before security gets to the door and takes Will to the lobby. Finally, two uniformed police arrive to take him to jail and book him for disturbing the peace.

"I thought you said your clients didn't know how to find you," Taylor said.

"They don't know about my private room several floors up, but I guess I have used this room too many times. There are security cameras in the lobby, elevators, and hallways. I stand in the hallway with my client at some point, so there is a video of us together. That way I have a picture of every client. That is my insurance if I have any problems with them."

"That sounds like a good plan, my darling, but it doesn't seem to be working with this Will. Maybe you need to get a better plan."

"You're probably right, but now that you're here, I won't have to deal with men like Will."

CHAPTER 34

On Friday morning, Nancy texts Steele to let him know the medical examiner completed the autopsy report on Bette Thompson.

"Hi, Doc, I understand you finished the autopsy report on Thompson."

"I just finalized the report. What do you want to know?" the medical examiner asked.

"What time did she die, and what killed her?"

"I estimate her death to be on Wednesday evening between 5:00 p.m. and 7:00 p.m. Although she was a smoker, she had an overdose of nicotine in her system. She had more than three times the expected nicotine of an average two-pack-a-day smoker. Nevertheless, she was alive when someone suffocated her, so I'm putting suffocation as the cause of death," the ME said. "Otherwise, she was about a forty-five-year-old woman, five foot four and weighed 143 pounds. Her lungs showed signs of emphysema and COPD. She also had coronary heart disease, but she should have lived for many more years. The woman was also eleven weeks pregnant."

"How do you know somebody suffocated her?" Steele asked.

"There was also petechial hemorrhaging of the eyes, which indicates asphyxia. I didn't find evidence that someone strangled the victim, and I also found a light blue strand of fabric in her nose, which probably matches a pillow at the scene. So, you'll know when you see the pillow. I will give you a picture of the strand."

"Thanks, Doc. So, I guess two people were trying to kill her."

"That's right. One is using poison, and the other one decides to smother her," the doctor said.

"I would also like a copy of the report when you have it," Steele said.

"Sure. I'll send it to your office today."

Steele heads to the therapy clinic to start a homicide investigation with his new information. First on the list will be Drew Spencer, owner of the building, and he was one of the people that discovered the body.

"Mr. Spencer, do you have a minute? I would like to ask you some questions."

"Of course, let's go to my office," Drew said.

"Did Miss Thompson have any enemies, or did you know anyone that wanted to kill her?"

"I thought Bette had a heart attack."

"No, this is officially a homicide, and I would like to look at her office again."

"Sure, we can go now, and you can ask all your questions in her office."

"Is this where you found her?" Steele asks.

"Yeah, she was on the couch."

"I'm going to take this pillow to the lab," Steele said as he put the pillow in a large evidence bag. "Did Miss Thompson have any problems with anyone?"

"No, the only person giving her grief is Will Hudson. He was the father of her baby, and he wanted her to get an abortion, but she refused," Drew said.

"What about Pete Rossi from the pizza shop?"

"I think Pete liked Bette, and he appears to be devastated by her death. Otherwise, everyone liked her. She was a nice lady."

"Thanks for all your help. Where is Will Hudson?" Steele asks.

"I don't know where he is now, but he called me from jail late Wednesday night and wanted me to get him out. I told him he had to wait until morning since it was so late."

"What time did he call you from jail? Did he tell you why the police arrested him?"

"Will said the police arrested him about 9:00 p.m. for disturbing the peace. He called me about midnight and said if I didn't bail him out, he would have to stay in jail until his arraignment in the morning. But as I said, it was too late to get him, and he would have to wait until morning."

"So, you don't know where he is?"

"No, I don't. He didn't come into work today, and he didn't call in either. But when he misses work, it usually means he found a hot game, as he calls it. So, he could be anywhere."

"If he shows up or calls, would you let me know?"

"Sure, but going from past history, I don't think he'll come to work today."

CHAPTER 35

On Saturday afternoon, Steele wants to talk to Will, and as he is driving around he eventually passes the therapy shop. He notices a lot of cars in the parking lot. He turns into the lot, taking one of the last spots, enters the building, and said he is surprised they were open on a Saturday.

"We were backlogged with our patients and decided we have to work a couple of Saturdays to catch up," Drew said.

"Is Will in today?"

"Yea, he is, but he may be in the back smoking," Drew said. "I'm sorry I didn't call you when he showed up this morning, but we had patients all day."

"That's okay. As long as I can talk to Will now," Steele said as he went through the shop and confronted Will in the alleyway.

"May I have a few minutes? I have a lot of questions to ask you."

"What do you want to talk to me about?" Will asks as they both go into the office.

"First, I have to read you your rights. You have the right to remain silent. Anything you say can and will be used against you in a court of law. You have the right to an attorney, and if you can't afford an attorney, the court will appoint one for you. Do you understand the rights I've just read to you?"

"Sure, I understand them. Why are you going to arrest me?"

"No, you're just a suspect in an attempted murder, and I have some questions for you," Steele said.

"What do you mean I'm a suspect? What does that mean? What kind of questions are you going to ask me? Are you accusing me of killing somebody?"

"Do you know anything about Miss Thompson's murder?"

"Why would I know anything about her murder? Wait, I thought she had a heart attack."

"No, Miss Thompson was murdered. She was also pregnant with your child."

"How do you know it was my kid?"

"We did a DNA test, and it came back to you."

"Wait, how did you get my DNA? No one has ever taken my DNA."

"When I took your coffee cup from your office for fingerprints, I also had them do a DNA test if we ever needed it," Steele said.

"You can't do that. It's illegal."

"Now, tell me, where were you on Wednesday night?"

"I was with my girl, Jasmine. You can ask her."

"Of course, I'll ask her. You said you were with her all night? I will need her phone number and address."

"She lives in the Cosmopolitan Hotel."

"I need to ask you. Did you kill Bette Thompson?"

"No, of course, I didn't kill her."

"I'm going to check on your alibi and confirm some other information. And I will be back if your alibi doesn't check out. Just don't leave town," Steele said.

CHAPTER 36

"Hi, my name is Erin Kelly, and I have an appointment with Mr. Spencer."

Allen, the tech, takes her to one of the tables and tells her to remove the knee brace so Drew can start his examination.

"Thank you for seeing me so soon, Mr. Spencer. My doctor said you were the best therapist in town, and I feel lucky to get an appointment to see you so quickly."

"Please call me Drew. We are very informal here."

"Okay, Drew. I appreciate you seeing me so soon, especially on a Saturday."

"We deal with several doctors. When one of them requests an appointment for their patient, we do our best to fit them in immediately. Now, tell me how you hurt your knee."

"I was running and stepped in a pothole. I initially thought I hurt my ankle, but the doctor said it was my knee. So, he gave me this brace to wear about a week ago. Since then, I've been resting my leg and keeping my knee as immobile as possible."

"Well, that was very good. The immobilization helped with preventing further damage. Now, let me measure the range of motion in your knee. Then we'll set up a therapy schedule for you using different equipment to build strength and flexibility in your leg and knee. This way, we'll see if there is any improvement after a few therapy sessions. You'll also need to be careful for a while and wear the brace for support, so you don't reinjure your knee," Drew explains.

"That won't be a problem."

As Erin exercises, she sees Will come into the room and acknowledges him.

"Hello, Mr. Hudson?"

"I don't know you. How do you know me?"

"My name is Erin Kelly, and I'm the hotel guest services representative at the Cosmopolitan Hotel. I've seen you come into the hotel many times, and on Wednesday, the police took you to jail," she said.

Embarrassed by her comments, Will leaves the building before his coworkers comment. Shortly after he leaves, Detective Steele arrives and asks to talk to Will.

"He just left the building, so he is probably out back for a smoke," Drew said.

Steele finds Will in the alley.

"I checked out your alibi, and Jasmine said you were there Wednesday, but she kicked you out early, giving you plenty of time to kill Miss Thompson. She also told me all the details on how you were trying to kill Miss Thompson with the nicotine. Also, the jar of No Pain Freeze found on the floor of Bette's office contained a high amount of nicotine. The staff at the Hands-On Therapy said you were the one to fill the jar of lotion."

"You're wrong. I didn't kill Bette."

"You had motive. You didn't want her to have your baby. You had an opportunity to kill her. Your alibi doesn't check out, and Jasmine told us how you told her your method of killing Bette. So, turn around, Will, you're under arrest for the attempted murder of Bette Thompson and her unborn baby," Steele said as he handcuffed Will, then read him the Miranda warning again.

"Wait, you said for the attempted murder. I told you I didn't kill Bette," Will said.

"No, you weren't the one to actually kill her, but you did attempt to kill her with the nicotine. That is why you're being charged with two counts of attempted murder," Steele said.

"Why two counts of murder?" Will asked.

"One count is for Miss Thompson, and the second count is for the unborn baby."

Steele happily takes Will to jail and charges him with two counts of attempted murder.

CHAPTER 37

Marshal Robert Nice meets Steele in his office to talk about William Hudson. He tells Steele that since Hudson was arrested for disturbing the peace, Steele must report to the local police that he is in the Witness Protection Program and continue to be protected. Nice explains that the government put Hudson into the program because he testified against the Don and received protection. The marshal then explains Hudson's real name is Frank Lamar, but no one can know his real name. Steele informs Nice that Hudson is now in the county jail for premeditated murder. The disturbing the peace charge is still pending, but he will notify the police of his continued protection.

The Saffarino brothers send their bodyguards to visit Will's ex-wife to learn his name. She was delighted to give her husband's name to the mob's two huge and ugly men. They assure her that she will no longer be bothered since they know the man who squealed on the Don is Will Hudson.

The bodyguards return and give their information to the brothers. Anthony Saffarino tells the men to find Hudson's home and where he can be found.

After many hours of research, the men return with the news that Hudson is currently in jail.

"We found out that he's in there on a premeditated murder charge for killing that dame in the beauty shop," one bodyguard explains.

"Let me think about this for a while, and then I'll tell you what to do with Hudson, but right now, just sit tight," Anthony said.

The Saffarino brothers decide to visit the jail to talk with the king of the gangs in the county jail. There is always one inmate who has control of most of the inmates in jail.

The twins give the king the green light for his flunkies in jail to snuff out Hudson and take their time doing the job. The twins want to make sure Hudson knows that his days in jail are numbered. They want him to suffer before getting a shiv in his gut.

A few days later, Detective Steele is notified that somebody attempted to kill his prisoner during a fight in the prison recreation yard. The guards couldn't determine how many inmates in the exercise area were involved in the attack.

Marshal Robert Nice is furious that somebody injured Will Hudson while in jail under his protection. He checks with the jail to find out why Hudson wasn't in protective custody in jail. The guards working the day Hudson was attacked were unaware that the prisoner was in the Witness Protection Program. Somehow the two guards returning from their separate vacations weren't given the information that Hudson should be kept in protective custody.

The jail guards tell Nice that Hudson wasn't killed because the jail knife was too small to damage any major organs. Also, the swift action of the guards getting the prisoner to the medical clinic kept him alive, so he didn't lose a lot of blood.

The guards assure Marshal Nice that his prisoner will be sent to a minimum-security prison, where he will be safe.

Ashley Parker wrote her newspaper story and gave all the details of how Bette Thompson was poisoned and suffocated. Her alleged killer was Will Hudson, a physical therapist assistant at the Hands-On Physical Therapy Place. The police arrested him, and he is in jail without bond until his trial. Also, the lengthy story told how the jail inmates attacked Hudson, but he is recovering in the prison medical clinic.

Reading the paper, Taylor talks to Jasmine about the killing.

"I thought you said that Thompson was killed with nicotine, but the paper said someone suffocated her. Did you have something to do with this?" Taylor asks.

Jasmine leaves the bedroom and goes into the sitting area of her hotel apartment.

"Why aren't you answering me?"

"Do you think I'm capable of killing her?" she asks a few minutes later.

"You told me how angry you were with her."

"Sure, I was angry with her. I'm glad Will told me he would kill her, which gave me the opportunity to finish the job. Something I have wanted to do since she left us stranded without any money."

"This doesn't sound like you, Jasmine. I thought I knew you, but I don't like this side of you," Taylor said.

"Please don't talk like that, Taylor. I'm the same as when we first met all those years ago. Now, let's go and talk to the twins to see if they will let me leave the mob so we can finally be together. I've dreamed of just being with you for years," she said.

"Right now, I'm not sure that I even want to be with you anymore. Jasmine, you are not the same. You don't even act or sound like the person I used to know. How could you have changed so much over time?"

"Please, Taylor, don't talk like that. I am the same person that you knew so long ago. I'm so happy that we are finally together again. I couldn't bear to lose you again. I'm sure we can work something out."

CHAPTER 38

Dick Morgan meets with Steele to tell him that the Boss, head of the Palatka Pythons, is coming into town.

"My source tells me the Boss will be in town next week with another of his guys called the Enforcer. They want to try to set up their business of selling drugs to the people in The Villages. The Boss thinks he will be able to set up a program to sell drugs even though his two former guys couldn't do it themselves," Morgan said.

"Did you set up a meeting time and place?" Steele asks.

"I thought the alleyway off of Seven Mile Drive would be a good location since it was the scene of the first murder," Morgan said.

"That will be a good spot. What time and day did you tell them?"

"I told them Tuesday right after sunset would be good. Is that okay with you?"

"That's good. Just don't tell anyone about this. I don't want an informant telling the Boss that this is a trap."

Steele feels this will be a good bust. Finally, he will have the Boss and another of his guys under arrest, and he can wrap up this serial murder case. He has two days to plan his action before he confronts them.

Tuesday finally arrives, and just before the sun sets, Steele hides in the alleyway shadow next to the large dumpster.

The sun sets, and it is dark before the Boss finally enters the alley.

"What are you doing here?" Steele asks the Boss as he jumps out of the shadow.

"I ain't doing anything wrong, so just leave me alone," The Boss said startled.

"I told you when I last saw you not to come back here, but here you are back and ready to sell drugs," Steele said.

"What makes you think I'm selling drugs?"

"My informant told me," Steele said as he pats down the Boss and finds a large bag containing several small cellophane baggies filled with a white substance.

"Until someone can test this, I'm assuming this is heroin. So, kneel down and lace your fingers behind your head," Steele said and walked behind the Boss to handcuff him. A large figure steps out from hiding in the alley and hits Steele over the head with a leather Billy club before he can put the handcuffs on the Boss. As Steele falls to the ground unconscious, a small figure quietly scurries from the other side of the alley and injects the deadly poison into the buttocks of the Enforcer, causing him to fall near the dumpster. The tiny figure then runs out of the alley and into the darkness.

With Steele and the Enforcer both on the ground, the Boss grabs his bag of drugs and takes off.

Not hearing from Steele, Morgan decides to check on the situation and finds Steele and another guy on the ground. He calls dispatch on his radio and tells them Detective Steele is down and to send an ambulance.

Nancy hears the call on her police scanner and hastily goes to the scene to discover Steele is nonresponsive.

"Oh, Grant, what happened?" she asks as she sits on the dirty ground and puts Steele's head in her lap. She slowly moves his hair off of his forehead. He is starting to come around and is delighted to see Nancy is there.

"It was nice of you to come down here for me. I'm glad you're here," Steele said.

The ambulance arrives. The paramedics put Steele on a gurney and take him to the back of the ambulance. Steele sits up and tells them that he is okay.

"Just tell me if the Boss is still here?"

"No, he's gone, but his Enforcer is dead. I've requested the medical examiner to come out and get the body since I'm here and can't get it myself," Morgan said.

"Nancy, get Jack Wagner out here to process the scene," Steele said.

"Grant, you have a gash on the back of your head, and you're bleeding. You were unconscious. You have to go to the hospital."

"I'm not going to the hospital. The paramedics can put a bandage on my head, and I'll be fine."

Wagner arrives to see Steele arguing with Nancy and the paramedics about going to the hospital.

"Hey, Grant, take it easy. I can take care of this myself," Wagner said.

"Once the medics finish with me, I'll be fine, but you can start processing the scene. At least with this body, we have more information than we did with the other murder victims."

Steele wins his argument with Nancy while the paramedics put a bandage on the back of his head.

Wagner starts an extensive examination of the body.

"This one has the same python tattoo on his arm and neck just like the others. This one also has a gun and drugs in his pockets and is wearing a heavy gold chain with a gold snake pendant hanging off the chain. He also has an ID card, which claims his name is Enforcer, and he lives in Palatka, but nothing else," Wagner said.

"The perp didn't have time to take anything off the body before leaving. I wonder if the perp made any other mistakes."

They comb the area carefully, looking for clues, when Steele notices a syringe in the overflowing dumpster next to the body. He quickly takes an evidence bag out of his pocket and manages to scoop the syringe into the bag without touching it.

"Hey, Jack. Look what I just found," Steele said as he handed the bag to Wagner to keep the chain of evidence intact.

"Take this to the lab for analysis and fingerprints. Maybe we'll get lucky. This might be the break in the case we need," Steele said.

CHAPTER 39

On Friday, Ashley returned home after work to find that someone had ransacked the apartment while she was out. Picking up the baseball bat kept by the front door, she is armed with the bat as she carefully checks the apartment to make sure the intruder is gone. Finally, making sure the place is empty, she calls the police to report a robbery.

Soon, Steele and Wagner arrive to take the robbery report.

"What are you doing here already?" Steele asks Ashley as she opens her door. He is surprised to see her.

"This is my apartment, and it's not my fault someone decides to make a mess in here."

"When did this happen?" Steele asks.

"My roommate works the afternoon shift, and she leaves about noon, and I just got home at 5:30, so it had to be between noon and 5:30, I would think," she said.

"Besides all the chaos, is there anything missing?" Steele asks.

"As far as I can tell. My computer is the only thing I've noticed missing, but I will check with my roommate when she gets home."

"There is evidence that someone picked the lock on the front door, but there aren't any other signs of forced entry. Also, there aren't any useable fingerprints, so they may have used gloves or just wiped down everything they touched on their way out," Wagner said.

"Since we have forced entry and your computer is gone, we have a burglary. Now, why would anyone want your computer?" Steele asks.

"I had a lot of information on there. I am an investigative reporter, and I'm currently working on a couple of stories. They took my computer, but I still have all my research. I keep all my notes on a thumb drive, which I keep on my key ring."

"Okay, here is my card if you find anything else missing. The police report for your insurance company will be ready in a few days. Now, we are going to canvass your neighbors to see if anyone saw anything or has a surveillance camera with a photo of the perp," Steele said as they left.

Checking with the neighbors, they don't find anyone that saw anything, and there aren't any security cameras taking pictures of the neighborhood.

"Looks like this is a dead-end. So, why don't we call it a night," Steele said.

"You're right. The break-in looks like it may be just a neighborhood kid with nothing to do, and we'll eventually find the computer dumped in a local garbage can," Wagner said.

Ashley decides to go back to the office to see if she can get another iPad to continue her work. She doesn't notice someone following her as she is driving to work. Another vehicle T-bones the passenger side of her white VW Beetle at the next intersection. Witnesses call 9-1-1. Soon, the ambulance arrives with the fire department. The firefighters use the Jaws of Life to extract Ashley from the crumpled vehicle. The paramedics are putting her on the gurney for transport just as Steele and Wagner arrive.

"Is it just one person in the car?" Steele asks. "Apparently it was hit-and-run since there isn't another car here."

"Just the driver, and she's in shock right now. The firefighters had to cut her out of the car. We have taken her to Memorial Hospital."

"Do you have an ID on her?"

"Sure, Steele. It's Ashley Parker. She's in bad shape and can't talk to you now. So, you'll have to wait until the docs have a look at her."

"Thanks. I'll go to the hospital after our investigation. Steele radios Nancy and tells her he needs a hook out here and make it a good one. We have a lot of debris in the middle of the road that needs to be cleaned up."

"Okay, Steele. Sending you the best tow truck on the rotation. He does a good job cleaning the roadway before he takes the vehicle."

Steele starts his accident report with the info from her car, then takes measurements and determines the direction of travel for both vehicles. He notices paint transfer from a black vehicle on the passenger side of Ashley's car. Steele then interviews witnesses that may have seen the crash. He quickly discovers a large black Cadillac Escalade hit Ashley's white VW Beetle. Some witnesses noticed the Florida license plate on the Escalade had a horse on it, but they were too far away to see any numbers.

Wagner takes pictures and then helps Steele collect damaged car parts from the road for later comparison.

"Isn't it a coincidence that the black Cadillac Escalade is involved with so many crimes lately? I don't believe in coincidences. I'll have to check how many Escalades are registered in the area with a horse county plate on it," Steele said.

CHAPTER 40

Now that Steele has one of the python necklaces from the last body, he can visit local pawnshops. After getting rejections from several shops, he goes to the last one on the list, located near Orlando.

"Have you seen anything like this before?" Steele asks, showing the necklace and his badge.

"Sure, someone came in here with two of them just recently. I thought the necklaces were stolen, but the FBI Stolen Articles File database didn't have them listed. So, I thought they were okay. I gave him $5,000 for both necklaces," the pawnbroker said.

"Do you have the info on the person that pawned the necklaces?"

"The first time someone came in with the necklaces, I had their info, but lost it. They appeared to be very valuable. I wondered why the guy was getting rid of them, so I made a copy of his Florida ID in case the police were interested, and I also have a security camera. I don't want any trouble with the police."

"What do you mean the first time."

"This is the second time someone came in with these weird necklaces. The first time the guy had six of them."

"Tell me what you did with the first six necklaces?" Steele asked.

After they didn't sell I sold them to a jeweler for the gold."

"The camera isn't beneficial since the person had a hat on, and he kept his head down," Steele mumbled after checking the footage.

"The copy of his ID was black, and you couldn't t make out anything on it, so I just threw it away," the pawnbroker said.

"Do you have any info on the first time?" Steele asked.

"As I said, I lost the info on the first necklaces. Are the necklaces stolen?" the pawnshop owner asked.

"Somebody took them off two dead bodies, and I want to talk to the person who pawned the items. Tell me, what did you do with the necklaces?"

"Like I said I kept them for a while, and when they didn't sell, I took them to a jeweler and sold them for the gold."

Discouraged, Steele goes back to the station to check with Wagner.

Did you get the result back from the lab on the syringe?" Steele asks.

"Well, the prints were smudged, but we have a partial that we're still working on trying to find a match. The lab reports show that Carfentanil or the brand name of Wildnil was in the syringe, just like the last two murders."

"So, all three murders are alike. I just wish the Boss didn't get away. How are we going to find him now?"

"You should have called the Palatka Police Department two days ago, and if he was back in town, they could arrest him for you. Then you go and get him," Wagner said.

"Thanks, Jack. I should have thought of that myself. I guess the blow to my head scrambled my brain, and I'm not thinking clearly yet, and I still have a bad headache."

"Maybe you should have that checked out. The paramedics did say you probably had a concussion. At least that is what Nancy is telling everyone."

After talking with Wagner, Steele decides that it would be beneficial for him to go to the emergency room if nothing else but to clear his head. The emergency doctors concur that he has a concussion since he was unconscious for a while, and Steele currently has a headache and admits to being confused.

They want to admit him into the hospital for a few days to rest and restrict his activities allowing his brain to recover. Steele promised the doctor that he would take a few days off if he didn't have to go into the hospital. "I don't like hospitals, and I promise you that I will take time off from my job to rest," Steele said.

"Okay, but to make sure you keep your promise, I'm going to talk to your chief to make sure he is aware of the situation."

"Okay, Doctor, I'll keep my word and stay home and do nothing for the next few days."

Several days later while resting, and mentally going over and over all the details in this drug case. Steele is ready to get back to actively solving this case. He starts with the medical examiner to find out the autopsy result on the third murder victim.

"Hi, Doc. Did you complete the autopsy?"

"Yes, Steele, and it is almost identical to the first two bodies. This one is six foot four and weighs 230 pounds. This one is a bit different because he has a muscular body and was taking performance-enhancing drugs, like steroids, so he was probably into bodybuilding. He also had a lot of heroin in his system. He is in his midtwenties and has severe lung damage. He also has inflammation of the nose's membrane, which caused a hole in his nasal septum, just like the others. There is significant heart damage probably caused by his heroin addiction, and he almost certainly would have been dead in a few years with all the drugs he was taking. He had an obvious puncture hole in his lower right buttocks probably caused by an injection, just like the others," the ME said.

"So, basically, he is the same as the other two murdered guys," Steele said.

"I can confidently say that all three men lived an addictive lifestyle, and all were murdered in exactly the same manner," the doctor said.

"Thanks, I figured that all the autopsies would be the same. Please let me know when you get the tox screen back, but I'm sure it will be like the first two."

With the third victim the same as the others, Steele is sure he is dealing with just one murderer. The cold cases involving murders in the alley had to be the same. The pawnshop owner claims to have bought and sold eight necklaces so that they may just be connected. This can't possibly be a coincidence because Steele doesn't believe in coincidences.

He is still puzzled on why the three men would come here just to sell drugs. They are probably already dealing drugs in Palatka, so the question is, why travel down here to sell drugs when it would be easier to just stay in their hometown. Could they possibly have a more extensive client base here to make a move profitable? He will have to call the Palatka Police Department, as Wagner suggested, to see if they know the Boss's location. *Wagner is right I should have called two days ago.* He doesn't have the time or desire to travel to Palatka. He hopes the Palatka police will find the Boss and transport him to Steele making life a lot easier.

This case has been confusing from the start, and he will be happy when he can put all the pieces together and figure it all out.

CHAPTER 41

Steele is not happy about visiting Ashley Parker in the hospital, but he has to interview her about the accident. He has not liked her since she first showed up at the scene at the Hands-On Therapy break-in. For some reason, their personalities clashed right from the beginning. Mumbling to himself, he wonders why she can't be more like Nancy. Then she would be pleasant, helpful, and supportive. But Steele considers himself a professional, knowing he should never let his feelings interfere with his work. There was one exception about a year ago when he almost killed the pedophile, but he feels that is different because, in his opinion, people that molest children should not be allowed on this earth. Now that Steele has transferred to this area, he hopes no one will learn of his undesirable past with his anger problem concerning pedophiles. After taking a deep breath, he enters Parker's room.

"Good afternoon, Miss Parker. You are looking well today."

"Thank you, Detective. I'm doing better, and I will be going home in a few days. I only have a broken leg and a lot of very painful bruises, but I'm starting to heal. I was lucky, and it could have been a lot worse. Did you see my car?"

"Yes, you were fortunate. Your car is totaled. Somebody pushed the passenger side door into the steering wheel. Do you remember anything about the accident that could help us?" Steele asks.

"To be perfectly honest, I don't remember anything. I was driving to work to get another laptop when someone struck my car, and that's all I remember," Ashley said.

"Do you know of any reason anyone would want to harm you?"

"As I told you before, I'm working on a couple of big investigations, which I will be happy to share with you soon, but not right now. So, I don't know if that helps you or not."

"No, it isn't very helpful. If you could share some information on your investigations, it would be of assistance. But right now, we don't have a lot of evidence to go on, but we're still working on it."

"Do you think someone did this on purpose?"

"Well, there is a possibility that someone wants you out of the way to stop your investigations," Steele said.

"Wait. Did you get my car keys from my wrecked car?"

"No, I don't think anyone removed anything from the car before the tow truck driver took your vehicle. So why are you asking?"

"As I told you before, I have a thumb drive with all the info on my stories, and I keep it on my key ring. It is essential to get my thumb drive back. Could you possibly get it for me since I won't get out of here for a few more days?"

"I'll get it when I inventory your car after I leave here," Steele said.

"Thanks, I really need that flash drive, and I appreciate you're getting it for me," Ashley said.

She then relaxes after being assured she will get her car keys back.

"One good thing about landing in the hospital is while I'm here, I can visit Chuck Vaughn. We're becoming friends."

"How are you becoming friends, and when did you meet?" Steele asks.

"Don't you remember I met Chuck when I interviewed him in the hospital after his beating? Of course, you weren't too happy to see me then either."

"Okay, I do remember."

"After the surgery to fix my leg, the nurse's aide took me to visit Chuck in a wheelchair. Now I'm doing pretty good on crutches and can get there myself. We will both be leaving the hospital soon and plan to take care of each other. He has multiple broken bones in his face and a broken right arm, and I only have a broken left leg, so we would make an excellent team to help each other recuperate."

"You are both vulnerable right now. So, be careful that you don't rush into anything you would later regret. Also, if someone is after you, do you realize that you're putting Chuck in danger too?" Steele said.

"Don't worry, we aren't moving in together, and we will be extra cautious about everything we do. We will just help each other with shopping and trips to the doctor, things like that. But thanks, Detective. I will keep your advice in mind."

CHAPTER 42

Jasmine makes an appointment with the Saffarino brothers. She is anxious to quit the mob connection so she can have an everyday life with Taylor. Jasmine has longed to be with Taylor, the love of her life, for many years. Now that he has found her, she is ready to put her past behind her.

The twin brothers are in the back of the deserted restaurant sitting in their customary red leather booth. The two enormous bodyguards are standing behind them as usual.

"Welcome, Jasmine. Why do you look so troubled? And who do you have with you?" the twins asked.

"This is Taylor Dalton. I told you about him some time ago. After all this time, he's found me. I would like you to allow me to leave the organization so I can be with him," Jasmine said.

"Jasmine, right now, we have exciting news. We're going legit."

"I don't understand. What do you mean you're going to be legitimate?"

"We've already agreed with the Seminole Tribe in Tampa. They have agreed to let us build a small casino in the back of our hotel, providing we don't have slot machines."

It is illegal to have slot machines in Florida except at the tribal casinos located on their reservations. The tribes may allow small casinos, which could offer Black Jack, Craps, Roulette, Poker, and Texas Hold'em, but not slot machines.

"The construction has already started and we're scheduled to open the casino in a few weeks and plan to have a big celebration for our grand opening. So, we want you to be present at the opening ceremonies with us," Pauli, the elder brother, said.

"Will I be able to leave after the grand opening?" Jasmine asked.

"I'm sorry, Jasmine, but we have to keep you and the other girls. You are our big money makers. We are also keeping our private high roller gambling games," Pauli said.

"Won't you be making a lot of money off the casino?" she asks.

"Sure, that's why we need you to stay. We'll be making a fortune and have to get rid of it, so we don't have to pay taxes on it. So, about every two to three weeks, one of the boys from the New York mob will come down here and win a couple of hundred thousand dollars or more. And you know they look forward to seeing you when they come down here. That way, we'll be getting rid of a lot of money and sending it to the mob in New York," Pauli said.

"Can't you make an exception for me? Other girls are working here too."

"We can't lose you, Jasmine. You are the most requested escort that we have. Sorry, but no one ever leaves the mob, and you will not be the first."

Disappointed, Jasmine thanks the brothers for their time and goes upstairs to her apartment.

"Now, what am I going to do?" she asks Taylor.

"Jasmine, you know you can't fight the mob. Besides, how did you get involved with them anyway?"

"After Bette left us without any money, we had nowhere to go. It seemed the mob just showed up and was there to help us, and that's how we started with them," she said. "They were willing to take care of us, and they relocated all of us girls to Florida. It has all worked out for me until now. Right now, all I want to do is leave all of this and go away with you."

"And how can you live with yourself knowing you killed Bette?" Taylor asks.

"Can't you see that I'm upset, and will you stop bringing up Bette's death?"

"Jasmine, when I met you, you were a very nice, caring young lady, and that is why I fell in love with you, but you are not the same. You have become coldhearted, and I don't like this side of you. But now I can see how you could have killed Bette."

"Taylor, please don't say that. I love you, and I can change and be the person you used to know. Just give me a chance."

"I'm sorry, Jasmine, I can't be with you knowing you're capable of killing someone. I'm leaving. Goodbye."

"Please, Taylor! Don't leave me! I need you!"

Crying, Jasmine falls onto the bed and sobs. Taylor takes his belongings and leaves, never to see her again.

CHAPTER 43

It had been a few days since Steele talked with Nancy, and he was nervous. Since he was a bit dizzy at the ambulance and not sure if she heard him say he was happy she was there with him. Steele doesn't feel ready to admit his feelings for her. So, he decides not to mention the incident and hopes she doesn't say anything either. Since he recently finished a destructive relationship, and isn't interested in starting anything new.

"Hi, Nancy, could you check how many black Cadillac Escalades are in The Villages?"

"There doesn't appear to be any black Escalades in The Villages. The ones listed are different colors. There are a couple of the black ones on the list, but they're in a different vicinity. Any special area you're looking in?"

"There can't be that many black Cadillac Escalades here. People in Florida usually pick lighter colors because of the blazing, hot sun. So, give me a list, and I'll check them all out," Steele said.

The printer noisily spits out the paper with five vehicles matching the description. Steele looks over the list and declares that he has found his car.

"This has got to be it. The registered owner is the Cosmopolitan Hotel LLC," Steele said.

This hotel was where a guest lost his license plate, which was later seen on the vehicle leaving the scene of Chuck Vaughn's beating and the car crash.

Steele decides to take Wagner along to look for evidence. They arrive and find the car in the parking lot, but it doesn't even have a scratch and it has a different plate on it.

Steele and Wagner search for the Saffarino brothers since they are the listed owners of the hotel. They ask the hotel guest services representative where they can find the owners. She tells them the brothers are in the restaurant just around the corner from her desk.

After being in the afternoon sun, the men squint as they enter the dark, empty restaurant, careful not to stumble over tables and chairs. They find the brothers in the back of the room, sitting in their red leather booth. Two enormous bodyguards are in attendance.

"Gentlemen, my name is Detective Grant Steele with FDLE, and this is CSI Jack Wagner. How many cars do you own?" Steele asks as he shows them his badge.

"We have two cars. A new black Lincoln Navigator and a new black Cadillac Escalade. Why are you asking?"

"Has your Cadillac Escalade been in an accident lately?" Steel asks.

"You can see for yourselves. The car is outside and is in mint condition," the twins answered in unison.

"Thank you for your time. We'll be back if we have other questions," Steele said.

"You are welcome here anytime, Detective," Pauli said.

As they leave the restaurant, Steele knows this is the car from the crash and connected to the beating. He has a gut feeling about it, and his gut is usually right. He just has to find some proof.

"Well, if the car was the one witnesses saw, they did have enough time to get it fixed from a body shop that works with the brothers," Steele said to Wagner.

"True, but if they did the work for the mob, they aren't going to be willing to talk to us."

"Well, we can check with a couple of body shops around here and interview them. Maybe we could catch a break."

"Sorry, Steele, I think they're more afraid of the mob than the cops. Maybe we can develop a different angle to prove they beat up Chuck Vaughn and were involved in Ashley Parker's crash."

"You're probably right. "We need to find that angle."

CHAPTER 44

Drew and Vicky have been talking about all the past few week's events and decided it was time to visit Chuck Vaughn and assure him that he will have a job when he is ready to go back to work.

"Hi, Chuck. How are you feeling?" Drew asks.

"I'm doing good. The doctors have agreed to let me go home tomorrow."

"Oh, that's wonderful," Vicky said.

The two tell Chuck that Will Hudson killed Bette. While in jail, the inmates tried to kill him while he awaited trial.

They continue telling Chuck that Larry Bellamy is working at the shop, but his job will be there for him when he can return. Since they have a lot of clients and Will is no longer embezzling from the business, they were able to keep Chuck on the payroll until he is able to go back to work. That's the right thing to do for a good friend and a loyal employee.

They explain that Larry graduated with Drew, and they reunited at the recent class reunion.

Drew assures Chuck that he has been with him since the beginning and will not let him down.

"A lot has happened since I've been in here. I feel bad that I can't thank Bette for saving my life when she screamed."

"Don't worry about that. We think Bette knew her screams helped you," Vicky said.

"Oh, I have to ask you. Do I get a discount on the cost of my therapy when I get out of here? The doctors said I will need several weeks of work to get my arm back to normal," he said with a smile.

"I'm sure we can work out some sort of employee discount."

They continue talking, and Chuck tells Drew that he is very superstitious and feels he is partly responsible for the beating. Chuck always wears his lucky shirt when playing poker with the other guys in a friendly neighborhood game. Then explains how there wasn't time to do his laundry, so he wasn't wearing his lucky shirt. Also, he remembers his grandmother's folklore that you never leave a place by a different door than the one you entered, or you'll have bad luck.

"Since I've worked with you, I always entered by the front door and left work the same way, even though I parked on the side of the building. It was a way to get exercise, but I was running late that night. Without thinking, I just went out the back door. I just feel better now, knowing they weren't after me but after some-one named Frank."

"Who wasn't after you?" Ashley asks as she enters the room on crutches.

"Detective Steele explained since the guys that beat me up kept calling me Frank, they mistook me for someone else.

"Drew and Vicky, this is Ashley Parker, a reporter for the *Chronicle*. We met for the first time in the hospital when she came to get an interview after the beating. We started talking and discovered we have a lot in common."

"Yes, I met you when you came to my therapy place asking for more information," Drew said.

"Ashley has set up transportation for me to go home tomorrow, and her roommate has already gone to my apartment several times and taken care of my cat. He was a stray, and I named him Lucky because I found him and gave him a good home," Chuck said.

"Thank you, Ashley, that is very kind of you to help Chuck," Drew said.

"We have become friends since we both ended up in the hospital. Chuck is a nice guy," she said.

"We both agree on that," Drew said.

"With my roommate's help, we'll help Chuck with his recovery. Hope-fully, we can get our therapy sessions simultaneously to drive to our appointment together."

"Now, if you plan on getting your therapy with us, we will be able to fit you in. Also, Vicky and I are here if you need help with anything, Chuck."

"I'm sure my roommate and I will be able to take care of Chuck and make sure he gets to all his appointments. Fortunately, I broke my lower left leg and only have a soft cast on, so I'll still be able to drive with my good right leg."

"That's wonderful, but please call if either of you needs assistance with anything. That is what friends do for each other," Drew said.

"Thank you. I'll keep that in mind," Chuck said.

On their way home, Vicky gets a call from her nephew, Hunter Langford.

"What is that all about?" Drew asks.

"My nephew Hunter wants to know if he can stay with us for a few weeks, and I told him we would meet him at the house in a few minutes," Vicky said.

"It's been at least a year since he was last here. I wonder why he wants to visit us now?"

"I'm sure he'll tell us all about it when he gets here."

Hunter arrives and gives his aunt and uncle a big hug.

"My goodness, you have certainly grown since we last saw you. You look like a movie star with your blond hair and blue eyes," Vicky said.

"Thank you, Aunt Vicky. I've recently had a growth spurt, and I'm now six foot four."

Hunter explains that his parents are on vacation in Paris for the next two months, and he feels the house in Greenwich is too big for just him. He thought this would be an excellent opportunity to spend some time in Florida visiting his family and getting together with the guys from his old gang. Drew and Vicky agree to let him stay in the guest room as he has done several times in the past.

They enjoy an elegant dinner of chicken parmesan with garlic toast and a mixed-greens salad all prepared by their nephew.

"You are a surprise. Where did you learn to cook like that? The whole dinner was delicious, and now you're clearing off the table. You have certainly matured since the last time you visited. I can't believe you're only seventeen."

"Thanks, Aunt Vicky. Last year, I spent some time with a chef, and she taught me everything I know about cooking."

"Well, she certainly taught you well. That was the best meal we've had in a long time. She must have cooked you healthy meals because you look like an athlete."

Hunter takes off his watch and turns up his shirt sleeves to wash dishes.

"What is that on your left inside wrist?" Vicky asks.

"Oh, it's just a tattoo that I got with the gang when I was last here."

"It's an adorable little gold crown. What does it stand for, and what does it mean?"

"It doesn't stand for anything. It's just a stupid thing all the guys did one day when we didn't have anything else to do."

"Well, I hope you don't plan on doing other stupid things while you're here. I want to stay friends with my sister."

"Don't worry, Aunt Vicky. I'll behave myself while I'm here."

Hunter washed the dishes and put the kitchen back to its previous spic-and-span condition. He remembers how his aunt and uncle have always been neat and orderly where everything had a place. He just wants to keep his aunt and uncle happy so he can continue to stay with them.

CHAPTER 45

Nancy sends a text to Steele informing him the tox results are in for the third murder victim, and the fingerprint results are back.

She gives him the report, stating the third victim had Carfentanil and a large amount of heroin in his system. The victim had enough heroin to show he was addicted to the drug.

Another report gives Steele the name belonging to the partial print found on the syringe belongs to Peter Rossi.

"I can't believe the prints came back to Rossi," Steele tells Nancy.

"Why are you surprised?"

"Because the kid is just very small, and he doesn't fit the profile of a serial killer. He appears to be just a nice little guy."

"But didn't you tell me the medical examiner said the killer had to be a woman or someone petite because of the way the perp put the needle into their butt?" Nancy said.

"You're right. I forgot about that. I guess it's time to visit Pete."

Steele stops at Tony's Pizza Shop, but Pete isn't there. Tony suggests he might be out back having a smoke and tells Steele to go out the back door to check on him.

Steele finds Pete sitting on the bench smoking a cigarette.

"Hi, Pete. Do you remember me?"

"Sure, you were there when Bette died."

"We found the syringe with your fingerprint on it and traces of the drug Carfentanil. I'm here to arrest you for killing three men with that drug."

"I've been waiting for you. Sure, I killed all the drug dealers for the money. But, now I have nothing to live for since Bette is gone."

"Okay, Mr. Rossi, stand up and put your hands behind your back," Steele says as he puts handcuffs on him. "I'm charging you with three murders in the first degree."

Steele reads the Miranda warning to Rossi and asks him if he understands his rights? After Rossi acknowledges that he does, Steele takes him to central booking.

The jailer pats down Rossi and has him remove his valuables plus his belt and shoelaces. The guard puts the articles in a large, clear plastic bag and gives him the receipt for the items. Next, another guard takes him for his mug shot and fingerprints.

After the guards finish the paperwork, Rossi is allowed to make a phone call and call his lawyer, Warren Wheeler. He makes the call and explains he is in jail on murder charges.

"Don't say anything to the police and be careful on this call. The jail telephones are not private, and they are probably recording this call. Remember, don't talk to anyone and tell the arraignment judge that you plead not guilty. Then I will arrange to meet privately with you later that day," Wheeler explained.

Pete stays in the county jail until his arraignment.

"You are being charged with three counts of first-degree murder. Do you understand the charges as they have been read to you?" the judge asks at the arraignment.

Pete acknowledges the charges.

"How do you plead to the charges? Do you have a lawyer?"

"I plead not guilty, Your Honor, and Warren Wheeler is my lawyer," Pete answers.

"You will have a preliminary hearing in six months. Since this is a murder case, you will be remanded to the county jail without bail until your hearing."

CHAPTER 46

On Tuesday morning a message is sent to Jasmine asking her to join the Saffarino brothers downstairs in the restaurant.

It has been several days since she's been out of her apartment, and she is not eager to go anywhere or see anyone.

"Jasmine, what is wrong with you? Your hair looks like a bird's nest. When was the last time you combed your beautiful hair? You look terrible."

The brothers continue talking to her, but she doesn't respond.

"You aren't working, and we're worried about you. So, we have arranged to have a psychiatrist go to your room and hold a two-hour session with you this afternoon. After that, you will go to his office to continue your sessions for your continued help until we get you back to normal. Do you understand?"

"Yes, I understand."

Dr. Adams arrives at her apartment to talk with her. He explains that he is there to help her since she is experiencing debilitating mental health symptoms that are interfering with her daily life. They talk, and the doctor gets Jasmine to remember her terrible childhood. She attended parochial schools in Detroit, and her parents were very religious, but that didn't stop the sexual abuse.

It didn't take long before she told Dr. Adams that her father molested her, and he always told her she was named Jasmine because she was his little flower. After months of being sexually molested by her father, she became pregnant at thirteen.

"I told my mother that it was my father that got me pregnant, but she couldn't believe her religious husband would ever do such a thing. She said I was sneaking out with a neighbor boy, and that is how I got pregnant. My mother said I was lying, and now I was no longer her daughter. Later, my father gave me $600 and told me to go to the Planned Parenthood Clinic in town the next day and get an abortion," she explained.

Jasmine completed the two-hour session and told the story about when her father gave her the money. She went to her room and emptied the little suitcase that held doll outfits and packed some of her own clothes.

With her small suitcase, the money, and her favorite tiny but worn brown teddy bear, she left her family home. She didn't have a plan when she sneaked out the bedroom window with her limited possessions. She only wanted to get as far away from her father as possible. Jasmine hitched a ride to the Greyhound bus terminal and purchased a ticket to Dallas, Texas, and still has money for food along the way.

Although she didn't have family in Texas, she always read about the cowboys and horses and decided that was the place to go. After two days of traveling on the bus, she was exhausted when she arrived in Texas. Jasmine was disappointed because she couldn't see any horses from the terminal, and she wondered if she had picked the wrong destination.

Looking tired and lost, Jasmine lay down on the wire bench, clutching her tattered teddy bear. A woman sat beside her and asked if she had a place to go. The thirteen-year-old Jasmine was naïve and explained to the kind woman why she had run away from home.

The woman, Bette Thompson, took the young girl to her brothel to live until the baby was due. Bette was like a mother to her.

While waiting for the baby to arrive, Bette taught Jasmine how to dress, put on makeup, fix her hair, and coached her about the sexual secrets to becoming a prosperous escort.

Jasmine went to the St. Mary's Children's Home to have the baby and put him up for adoption. Knowing her child would be adopted by a young couple helped Jasmine cope with the agony of giving up her child.

It only took six weeks of strenuous exercises for Jasmine to lose her pregnancy weight and turn herself into a voluptuous and shapely woman.

It didn't take long before the young Jasmine became the star of Bette Thompson's Escort service in Dallas, Texas.

Jasmine could not believe how her long-held secret just came tumbling out. She felt lighter, like someone had taken a load from her shoulders. The doctor assured her this was normal for someone with a mental burden to release its hold with the help of a professional psychiatrist. He also prescribed an antidepressant to help her cope.

"We are only at the beginning of your treatment," the doctor told her. "But we made a lot of progress today."

"Thank you, doctor, and I do feel better."

"We will make even more progress at the next session in my office."

CHAPTER 47

After Pete Rossi's arraignment with the circuit judge, the correctional officers take him back to the county jail to wait for his court date and to plan his defense with his criminal lawyer, Warren Wheeler.

The six-foot-tall Mr. Wheeler is wearing a pinstriped double-breasted suit with a light gray dress shirt and a charcoal tie that fits a successful lawyer's image as he enters the small, stuffy interrogation room without windows. The private room is secure so a lawyer can confidentially talk with his client. He sits at a metal table and opens his well-oiled leather briefcase, removing his fountain pen and legal pad in preparation for the interview.

Rossi shuffles into the room wearing the orange jumpsuit the Department of Corrections provided with handcuffs and shackles on his legs with the guard at his side.

"Pete, you look pale. Are you feeling okay?"

Rossi sits on the metal chair, rubbing his wrists after the guard removed the handcuffs and left.

"Yeah, I'm doing okay."

"Good, now, Pete, tell me everything that happened when Detective Steele arrested you."

Pete relays all the details of his arrest to his attorney. He also tells him how he confessed to the detective, and said that he did kill the men for money. Since his family was gone, he didn't have a reason to go on living, and he didn't care if the detective was going to arrest him.

"When did you tell the detective that you killed the men?" Wheeler asked.

"The detective came outside while I was smoking and said he was going to arrest me for the murders. I then told him that I was guilty and had been waiting for him," Rossi said.

"Did the detective read you your Miranda rights?"

"Yeah, he did."

"This is important now. Tell me exactly when the detective read you your rights?"

"After I told him that I was the killer, he handcuffed me and read me my rights."

"Are you absolutely sure that you confessed before he read you the Miranda warning?"

"Yes, I'm sure, but what difference does it make?"

"It makes a lot of difference. Now, we can throw out your confession since you confessed before the detective read you your rights. That is very important. I'm sure the district attorney is not going to be happy with this information. Okay, Pete, I only want to know about the evidence or information that the prosecution will know about so I can plan your defense. So far, the only evidence against you is a partial fingerprint on the syringe and your confession."

"It doesn't matter. With Bette and the baby gone, I have no reason to live. They were my whole life," Pete said.

"You have to stay focused on your defense. So, the confession is no longer valid, and the partial fingerprint can also be thrown out because I can argue that there won't be enough of the print to prove it's yours. Now, is there any evidence to connect you to these killings?"

"No, all the communication I had with everyone involved and my searching for a way to kill someone was all on the internet. After the last murder, I destroyed my computer by burning it in my backyard burn pit. I then took the remainder of the computer to the dump."

"So, there won't be any surprises from the district attorney at trial? Is that right?"

"As far as I know, there isn't anything that will connect me with all the murders," Rossi said.

"We are finished today, but remember, don't talk to anyone without me present. This is very important. Do you understand?"

"Sure, but what difference does it make?"

"Remember, just because you confessed doesn't mean it's true. The court says you are believed to be an innocent person until you're proven guilty of the crime. You are not legally guilty until the prosecution offers enough evidence to persuade a judge or jury to convict you of the crime. Now, don't tell me anything about the alleged murders. I can't present anything that I know to be false to the court. Do you understand? I can't allow you to testify to your innocence if I know you're guilty."

"Yes, sir, I understand, but could you do me a favor?"

"Sure, what can I do for you?"

"I want you to arrange a beautiful funeral for Bette. I have plenty of money in my checking account to cover whatever it'll cost. Use the rest of the money for your fee and give anything left to charity ."

"I will take care of the details. The next time I come, I will bring your checkbook and you can make out the check to the funeral home," the lawyer said. "I will stay in contact with you."

CHAPTER 48

After being out of town for about a year, Hunter visits with his Privileged gang at their large house just outside of The Villages on Tuesday morning. Edgar Fellows is currently in charge of the house and its members.

"It has been a long time since your last visit," Edgar said, hugging Hunter. "It's good to see you. We have a lot of exciting news to tell you."

"Right now, the news can wait. Why isn't everyone in school today?"

"It's okay. We don't go to school. It's too boring, so we just stay home, take care of the business, and watch TV."

"Didn't I tell you before I left that everything had to stay the same? That meant everyone went to school every day or studied to get their GED? Otherwise, you'll have a Truant Officer ringing the doorbell to find out why you guys aren't in school, and you don't want that to happen," Hunter said.

"You're right. I let the younger boys skip school, not thinking about them being truant. We'll get that straightened out immediately, and I'll have the boys going back to school tomorrow."

"Okay, that also means you have to go back to school tomorrow too."

"It's okay. I was expelled last month for not following the rules."

"While I'm here, I'll get everything straightened out and make sure you get back into school. You're only fifteen, and I thought you were mature enough to handle the business, but I guess I was wrong."

"I'm sorry, Hunter, I wasn't thinking. I can take of everything. Give me another chance," Edgar said.

"Okay, we'll talk about this later. Now tell me how the business is doing?" Hunter asks.

"It's really doing well. Word of mouth from our satisfied customers is helping us a lot. We're getting more and more customers every day. You were right setting up business in The Villages. It's been very successful," Edgar said.

"That's great. Are you still able to get enough drugs from Cuba?"

"We are getting more than we can sell. So, we always have enough product for our customers. Many older folks want soft drugs like valium, tranquilizers, and sleeping pills. Also, since you've been gone, we've found a market for hard drugs like Oxycontin, Rohypnol, and Ecstasy. We also have a lot of people showing interest in our new product of adulterated cannabis."

"What is this new product you're selling?" Hunter said.

"The contaminated cannabis has synthetic cannabinoids that have human-made mind-altering chemicals sprayed on the dried, shredded plant material so it can be smoked or sold as a liquid for the e-cigarettes making it more potent. We just have to be really careful with this new drug. We have to use disposable gloves when packaging, selling, or handling the cannabis because it can be easily absorbed through the skin," Edgar said.

"You have to be careful. If you have too many products to sell, you'll only bring attention to us. That's why I started the business with only a few soft drugs to keep the old folks in The Villages happy, and it was sufficient to keep us filthy rich. Now, with more people buying the hard drugs, there'll be a greater chance of someone overdosing, and that will only bring the cops sniffing around looking for the source of the drugs. You really don't want the DEA to start looking at our operation. Besides, with more people using, they'll start talking to others. Before you know it, we'll also have drug dealers trying to push us out and take over our business."

"Don't worry, Hunter. We have someone willing to take out our competition as soon as they show up."

"What are you talking about. How are they getting rid of our competition? I thought everything was fine when I left."

"Right, you had everything set up before you were gone, but things changed as soon as you left."

"What do you mean things changed? What changed?"

"We will admit you had the business up and running smoothly. But right after you left, we had some drug dealers come here from out of town, and we had to find someone to get rid of them."

"What do you mean you had drug dealers come here from out of town?" Hunter asked.

"We found the Palatka Pythons wanted to sell their drugs in The Villages because they heard there were a lot of old folks looking for drugs, and they wanted to take over our operation. They were trying to sell heroin to our customers, and we had to stop it."

"How did you know who they were and wanted to sell heroin?"

"That was easy. The Palatka Pythons actually came to our house and said they wanted to make a deal to take over our business. So, we had to get rid of them."

"Please, explain how you got rid of them?" Hunter asked.

"The boys and I went online looking for a person to eliminate the outsiders, and we found a guy willing to do this for a price. We handled everything through the internet, and we never had to meet him."

"Well, isn't that great? How is this person handling the elimination of our problem?"

"We didn't ask how he did it. We just told him we wanted the Python gang gone, and he took care of it."

"How did you know they were gone?"

"We read in the paper and heard on TV that gang members were killed in the alleys; then we sent payment to our guy."

"How did you send payment, and to whom?"

"We use Western Union online payment, and he gives them our agreed-upon password and collects the money. It's that simple," Edgar said.

"Where did you get the money to pay him?"

"We used the profits from the business to pay him."

"Okay, how many gang members came here that you had to get rid of, and you're sure they aren't coming back?"

"Well, we have nine gang members eliminated, and I don't think there can be many more guys in the gang," Edgar said.

"I can't believe that you guys had nine gang members killed. How can you live with yourselves?"

"We didn't have a choice. We had a problem, and we didn't know how to reach you for advice, so we all talked it over, and this is the decision we made."

"I just hope you didn't leave any evidence so the cops can trace it back to this house, or we're all in trouble."

"I told you we did everything online and never met the guy. So, we're good."

"Did you tell him your name?"

"No, of course, we didn't do that. We set up a special email to talk to each other."

"I'm disappointed in you. I thought you could handle the business without getting in trouble."

"Don't worry, Hunter, we aren't in trouble."

"At least not yet."

CHAPTER 49

With Will Hudson out of the picture, the financial statements are starting to look better, and the Hands-On Therapy business is doing very well. Vicky was able to pay off all the past-due bills, and filing for Chapter 11 has helped them reorganize their debts and work out a payment plan, which has been successful in getting the business out of the red.

Drew decides it is time to gather his staff before they all go home and explain why they had to go a month without a paycheck in the past.

"I told you that I would explain the problems we were having. First, I want to thank all of you for being loyal to me when you had to wait a month before you started receiving your regular paychecks again. I hesitate to tell you this, but Will was embezzling money from the business to the point that I had to file for a Chapter 11 to stop the mortgage company's foreclosure. I asked you to go without your paycheck for a month because we just didn't have any money to pay you. We were so far in debt that it took us all this time to get our heads above water. Because you guys have been loyal to us, there will be a small raise in your next paychecks. Thank you again for your loyalty. Vicky and I couldn't have succeeded without your support."

"Thanks for the raise. I'm sure everyone can use the extra money," Larry Bellamy said.

Drew also explains that Chuck Vaughn is doing well, but won't be back to work for another couple of months.

"As you have seen, Chuck and Ashley Parker have been coming here for their therapy sessions, and they are both improving. Ashley is doing well enough to stop her therapy this week. She will continue to bring Chuck until he can drive himself," Drew said. "I'm sorry to tell you because you all know him, but Pete Rossi was arrested for murder. Unfortunately, that is all I know about the case."

The employees are all talking about their raise, and the shocking news Drew told them about Will Hudson and Pete Rossi. Detective Steele enters the office while everyone is still gathered around. "Sorry to barge in without calling first, but I have a few questions to ask everyone."

"You're welcome here any time," Drew said.

"Thank you. I wanted to know if anyone here was a friend of Pete Rossi?" Steele asked.

"I don't think anyone here really knew Pete. Will was the only one that was outside smoking with him and Bette. No one else here smokes. So, we didn't have an opportunity to talk with him," Larry said.

"I'm trying to find out anything I can about Pete. Does anyone know where he lived or anything about him?"

"Why don't you ask Tony? He should have all that information," Drew said.

"Tony doesn't have any information about Pete. When he hired him, Pete never gave him an address or phone number, and Tony didn't ask him for any information."

"Can you tell us anything about the murders or why you think Pete killed anyone? We're all very curious," Drew said.

"I'm sorry we can't talk about an open case," he said. "Thank you for your time. If you think of anything that would help, give me a call."

As Detective Steele leaves and everyone is still talking, Vicky's phone signals a message from Hunter saying he will not be home tonight as he is staying overnight with his buddies.

"That's strange. Hunter is not going to be home tonight. He always spends dinner with us when he's here. I wonder what he's up to with his friends?" Vicky asks Drew.

"He's a good kid, and I wouldn't worry about him. He just graduated from high school a year early, so I would think he's smart enough to stay out of trouble. Besides, he hasn't seen his friends for a while, and they probably have a lot of catching up to do," Drew said.

"Since we don't have Hunter at home tonight, why don't we go out to dinner?" Vicky said.

"That sounds like a great idea, and while you were checking your phone, some of the guys already said they want to go out to dinner with us. Since we gave them so much information today, they just want to keep talking about it," Drew said.

"Dinner out with the guys will be good for all of us. I just wish I knew what Hunter was doing?" Vicky said.

"Now stop worrying about him, and let's just enjoy dinner with the guys. Hunter is a responsible young man and can take care of himself."

CHAPTER 50

After taking the antidepressant and going to several sessions with Dr. Adams, Jasmine is doing better.

Dr. Adams helped Jasmine remember her terrible past, and with the doctor's help, she understands that killing Bette was causing her overwhelming anxiety. Her anxiety wasn't due to Taylor Dalton leaving her as she first thought. All her religious training from her childhood caused her to feel guilty for killing Bette. Her memory also revealed that she didn't kill the baby she was carrying when her father gave her money to have an abortion. She had forgotten that Bette was more of a mother to her than her biological mother. Jasmine just remembered how she wanted revenge for being stranded in Texas.

Talking to the doctor, she remembered everything from her past, which helped her understand her mental distress. The doctor explained that she was suffering an emotional response to the experience of the memory that Bette left her when she was vulnerable.

She now understands why she stopped taking care of herself and had the overwhelming doom of wanting to kill herself, but her religious background kept her from trying.

She remembered how she couldn't kill her baby, and knew killing Bette was wrong even though she knew Bette was on her death bed.

Dr. Adams explained she might feel better if she tried to find the son she gave up for adoption seventeen years ago and try to reconcile with him. Giving her purpose in life would be suitable for her now. He suggested she try social media, DNA testing sites, and the mutual consent registry in her attempt to find her son.

Feeling better about her situation, Jasmine starts her quest to find her son.

She doesn't know that her son has also been trying to find her for the last couple of years. It takes a lot of time to discover the son's name that she gave away. After checking social media, the DNA sites, and the mutual consent registry, she learns her son is Hunter Langford. He lives in Greenwich, Connecticut, with his parents, Mary and Jonathan. She is excited to find him, but wants to prepare herself mentally before contacting him. She doesn't want anything to go wrong with her first time visiting her son, Hunter.

The Saffarino brothers send a message for her to meet them in the restaurant.

"Oh, you look absolutely gorgeous today. Your hair looks great. We are glad you're on the mend. Dr. Adams told us you've greatly improved."

"I am feeling much better, and I want to thank you both for finding Dr. Adams for me. He has helped me a lot."

We're pleased to see you're doing better. Your clients are also happy that you're back to normal too. And the contractors will be finished with the casino tomorrow, and we want you to be there for the grand opening," the older brother said.

Jasmine got back into her routine but changed the method of dealing with her clients. Jasmine doesn't want to have the same problems she did with Will Hudson. She now uses a different room for each customer when they call for an appointment.

Jasmine keeps a journal with the names of her Johns, the date she saw them, and which room they used. She also insists they pay upon arrival at the front desk or security would be called, and they will not be allowed into the room.

Will Hudson caused her a lot of trouble, and she is taking a lot of precautions to protect herself from any future problems. If nothing else, Jasmine learned a lot from dealing with Hudson.

After learning the location of her son, Jasmine talks to the brothers again and tells them about her good news.

"Now that I know how to find my son, I would like to take a few days off to meet him," Jasmine said.

"Sorry, Jasmine, you can't leave now. We need you for the casino opening tomorrow. We expect several New York mob lieutenants to come down here, and you know how they look forward to spending time with you."

"I have been with you for several years and have never taken any time off for a vacation. I know I took a few weeks off when I was mentally ill, but that is all."

"Maybe in a few months, we can let you go for possibly one week. Would that be okay with you?"

"Do I have your word that I will be able to visit my son if I stay here now?"

"You have our word. In a couple of months, you can go."

"Okay, then I'm looking forward to the casino's grand opening. It will be exciting."

"Good, because we're happy you'll be with us as we start this new adventure," they said.

Jasmine is excited about finding the name and location of her son and calls Dr. Adams to share her good news. The doctor warns her that she could be disappointed. There could be many reasons your son may have changed his mind since he signed up with the mutual consent registry.

"Jasmine, just don't get your hopes up and prepare yourself for the worst outcome. You know you can call me anytime if you have any problems," Dr. Adams said.

CHAPTER 51

Dick Morgan meets with Steele to tell him about his clients. They go to their usual neighborhood coffee shop, and as they enter, Steele tells the waitress they would like two cups of coffee. They go to a back table for privacy and wait for their coffee before starting their conversation.

The last time they met, Morgan couldn't reveal the name of his clients because of the confidentiality clause. He explains to Steele that he can now break the confidentiality rule because there is a threat of harm to the people involved. That is the only way he can legally reveal his client's name.

"In the few years I've been a PI, I never gave up the name of my clients. So, this will be the first time for me."

"I understand. Can you give me the name now?"

"Sure, my client's name is Edgar Fellows, and I believe he and the minor children in the house are selling drugs to the elderly people in The Villages."

"Do you realize what you're saying? Children selling drugs?" Steele said shocked.

"First, let me tell you the story, and then you can ask questions."

"Okay, but you'll need proof for your accusations," Steele said.

"Of course, I have proof. Fellows first contacted me and gave me his email. Then, he told me he wanted me to tell him when any drug dealers came into town or if I heard of any drug activity in the area. I thought his request was unusual, so I watched his house and noticed several young boys didn't attend school. So, I continued watching and followed some of them, and that is when I discovered it appeared the kids were selling drugs to the folks in The Villages."

"Okay, where is the house that allegedly has minors selling drugs?" Steele asks.

"It's at 8328 Seven Mile Drive, just off Long Key Drive. It's the only two-story house on the road, so you can't miss it."

"Did you see the kids selling drugs to the elderly?"

"Yes, I couldn't believe it, so I took a lot of pictures."

"Good. Do you have the pictures with you?"

"Of course, here is the proof," Morgan said as he handed Steele the thumb drive with the incriminating pictures of the youngsters.

"Could you figure out what kind of drugs they were selling?"

"No, I didn't get close enough to see the kind of drugs they were selling, but it would be easy to find out."

"On some of the pictures, it is obvious they're selling some kind of pills," Steele said.

"After discovering their illegal activities, I checked the house and its occupants with the local police department. They told me the boys living there are between the ages of twelve to fifteen and belong to a group of boys called The Privileged. They have an older boy in charge of all the kids. It is more like a fraternity than an actual gang, and all the members have a small gold crown tattooed on the inside of their left wrists, which they can easily hide with a watchband," Morgan said.

"Did the police seem to be aware of their alleged drug dealing?"

"No, the police appeared to be proud of how the members acted like little gentlemen. They also said the boys were all very wealthy kids from prominent families and never caused any trouble for anyone. None of them have a criminal record."

"Did you tell them that you found the boys dealing drugs?"

"No, I wanted to talk to you first and see what you wanted to do with this information."

"Well, first, I think we should notify the Drug Enforcement Administration and give them your findings and evidence. They are the experts in finding and stopping drug activities."

Steele notifies the DEA, and an agent goes to Steele's office for the information and the evidence.

"This looks like an interesting case. The photos document their actions and tell an interesting story. In the fifteen years I have been with the DEA, I have had several cases where adult drug dealers have kids selling drugs, but this is the first time that minors have started their own business selling drugs," DEA Agent Gary Graham said.

The DEA agents obtain a warrant to search the house and drive to the address to collect the evidence. At the same time, Edgar Fellows calls 9-1-1 and tells the operator he needs help.

"What is your emergency?" the operator asks.

"I think my friend took too many pills. He needs an ambulance."

"What is your address?" the operator asks.

"We are at 8328 Seven Mile Drive. Please hurry. He doesn't look like he is breathing."

"Do you know how to do CPR?" the operator asked.

"No, I don't know how."

"Okay, let me tell you how to perform CPR. First, make sure he is lying flat on the floor."

"No. No. I can't do this. Just send an ambulance and hurry."

"Okay. The ambulance is on the way and should be there soon. Just stay with me. Don't hang up the phone."

"I can hear the sirens. Okay. They just pulled into the driveway."

"Alright, I will let you go to talk to the paramedics. Also, the police will be there shortly."

"He took too many pills," Fellows tells the paramedics as they enter the house.

The paramedics check for a pulse and do not find one, and one paramedic starts CPR.

The other paramedic administers Narcan. A minute after receiving the drug, the patient gasps and starts breathing, and the paramedics stop CPR. The patient is put on the gurney and taken to the ambulance.

"You will be fine. Just stay still while I put in an IV line and set up the oxygen. Do you remember what you took and how much?"

"I just took a couple of oxy pills," the patient said.

"Just try to relax while we take you to the hospital so the doctors can take care of you," the paramedic said.

The DEA agents arrive at the home as the ambulance leaves. The agents give the warrant to Fellows and begin searching the house and collecting evidence.

CHAPTER 52

Ashley Parker calls the police station and makes an appointment to meet with Steele about an important matter.

"I'm glad you made the time to see me. I won't be wasting your time."

"Have a seat and tell me what this is all about," Steele said.

"First of all, I want to thank you for going to the impound lot to get my key ring and thumb drive from my totaled VW. My office sent over a computer and I was able to finish writing my story while still in the hospital. I appreciated your efforts, and I wanted you to be the first to know about the big story I'm working on now."

"Why are you telling me this?" Steele asks.

"The Financial Crimes Enforcement Network has two mob members investigated for money laundering. I have written a three-part story all about it, and the first part will be in today's paper."

"Why do you think this is of interest to me?" Steele asks.

"You did promise me the scoop on the murders, which will help my career, and I thought if you knew about this before everyone else, it might help you somehow."

"Okay, this is interesting. Is it the Saffarino brothers that are under investigation?"

"Yes, how did you know?"

"It's simple. The brothers are the only mob guys in the area. So how were you able to discover this?"

"I have my informants, and I did tell you about my investigative stories that I was working on a few weeks ago. The Financial Crimes Enforcement Network works in the US under the authority of the US Treasury, and they investigate money laundering. I've been working with them and the FBI agents for several weeks after the casino opened."

"How were you able to get this evidence?" Steele asked.

"After the mob opened their casino last month, I gave the agents the information my informant gave me, and they just started to watch the casino and the brothers," Ashley said. "When the agents noticed more mob members going to the casino, they set up wiretaps to get the dirt on them."

"With the testimony from the informant, the Saffarino brothers will be going away for a long time. The wiretap also gave the FBI incriminating evidence about the New York mob coming down here and taking the money back up north," Ashley said.

"Well, I'm impressed with your work. You have surprised me with your professionalism," Steele said.

"Thank you, Lieutenant Steele. That means a lot to me."

"I'm curious about the identity of your confidential informant," Steele asks.

"Oh, Erin Kelly gave me the information so I could do my investigation. You remember her. She's the hotel guest service representative at the Cosmopolitan Hotel, and her desk is just a few feet away from the small restaurant the brothers used as their office in the hotel. When they talked in there, she told me that all the sound echoed out the door, and she heard everything."

"Why would Erin talk to you instead of the police?"

"Oh, that's simple, Erin is my roommate, and we have been friends for years."

Ashley Parker's first part of a three-part story appears in the *Village Chronicle*.

Jasmine reads the story about the FBI arresting the Saffarino brothers because they're involved with money laundering. Jasmine contacts the newspaper to get in contact with Ashley.

Ashley calls Jasmine to find out how she can help her.

"Miss Parker, I want to know how to reach the FBI. Can you help me?" Jasmine asks.

"Of course, but why do you want to reach them?"

"I can help them if they need any more information about money laundering."

"How can you help?" Ashley asks.

"I was there when they were talking about doing everything. I was in the room when the brothers explained to the mob lieutenants how they would launder the money. I was also there when the brothers gave the money to the mob."

"That is great. I will have the agent I've been working with give you a call. Will that be okay with you?"

"Sure, but I have to be careful. I don't want the twins to know that I'm talking about this, or they will have the mob kill me."

"I'm sure the agent will make all the arrangement to get you out of the hotel so he can safely talk to you."

Ashley tells the FBI agent about Jasmine's willingness to provide evidence, and is willing to testify in court, but she fears for her life. After hearing the information that Jasmine is willing to testify in court, the FBI knows her testimony's value, and they offer her the opportunity to enter the Witness Protection Program. Jasmine readily accepts their offer and considers this the perfect way to finally get away from the mob. Now she can start a new life and maybe spend time with her son in Connecticut.

The FBI immediately puts Jasmine in a safe house until she can go to court and testify.

With Jasmine having witnessed the illegal activities and willing to testify, the FBI no longer needs the informant's testimony. With Jasmine's help, the FBI's case is strong enough to get a conviction.

CHAPTER 53

Vicky received a call from Memorial Hospital notifying her that Hunter was in the Emergency Room. Her nephew was treated in the ambulance with Narcan because it was a life or death situation, but since he is a minor, he can't be treated in the emergency room until Vicky comes to the hospital with a medical consent form.

"Drew, Hunter is in the hospital. I have to go to him. Will you take me?"

"Of course, you're too upset to drive. What is Hunter doing in the hospital?"

"I don't know. The nurse just said he was in the Emergency Room, and they can't treat him until we give them the consent form from my sister."

In the past, her sister authorized them to care for her son if needed because Hunter stayed with them on several occasions.

Drew and Vicky arrive at the hospital, and they are told Hunter overdosed, but he should be fine since he was able to give his aunt's phone number as his emergency contact to the hospital.

Vicky calls her sister in Paris to tell her the bad news and assure her that Hunter is okay. Mary and Jonathan Langford charter a jet to get them to their son as quickly as possible.

Vicky explains to the doctor that Hunter probably took the pills because he was in pain. She explains that Hunter was in a severe car accident three years ago and suffered back and neck injuries. He was driving too fast in his Corvette and crashed into a tree. He has been on pain medication since the accident, which may be why he took the Oxycontin.

After talking to the doctor, Drew and Vicky are told they can see their nephew.

"Hello, Hunter. Oh, you look pale. How are you feeling?" Vicky asks.

"I'm a little shaky right now, but I'm feeling a little bit better."

"Your parents are on the way and should be here by tomorrow morning, and they are not happy about your overdosing."

"Oh no. Why did you have to tell my parents?"

"You know I had to tell them. As it is, your mom is already upset with me. Where did you find the drugs? Did you buy them?"

"Of course, I didn't buy them. The pills were in the medicine cabinet, and I didn't realize they were stronger than the ones the doctor prescribed for me. I didn't know they were so powerful."

Nancy notifies Steele and tells him there is an overdose at Memorial Hospital, possibly connected to the DEA case he is currently working. He heads to the hospital to find Drew and Vicky at Hunter's bedside, comforting their nephew.

"Detective Steele, this is my nephew Hunter Langford. His parents are flying in from Paris and will be here in the morning. In the meantime, we're staying with him. Since we have his medical consent form, the hospital said they would release him to us when he's feeling better."

"Hello, Hunter. Can you tell me how you got the drugs?" Steele asks.

"Sure, I found them in the medicine cabinet and didn't realize they were so strong. I already have a prescription for Oxycontin from my doctor for back pain, but I ran out and needed to get a refill."

"Are you saying you're addicted to Oxycontin?"

"No, I can stop anytime I want. I only take the pills occasionally when the pain gets too bad."

"Where were you when you found the drugs?"

"I was at the house with the other guys."

"Is that the house on Seven Mile Drive?" Steele asks.

"Yeah, how did you know?"

"Right now, the DEA has a warrant and is at the house collecting evidence."

"What is the DEA? And what are they doing at the house?" Vicky asks.

"The DEA is the Drug Enforcement Administration, and they are investigating the selling of drugs from that house," Steele said.

"Oh, no. Hunter. What is going on? Is this true?"

"Don't worry, Aunt Vicky. All this is a big mistake."

"Why would they say you're selling drugs? You have enough money to do whatever you want. I don't understand."

"No, you don't understand. We don't have a lot of money. It seemed all the parents of the kids in the house got together and decided we were all spoiled rotten. So, they decided to try tough love by taking away our money and only giving us a small allowance. We couldn't live on that, so we came up with a business to make money."

"I can't believe this," Vicky said, her hand covering her mouth.

The doctor enters the room and advises Hunter to stay twenty-four hours in the psychiatric ward since he tried to kill himself and the paramedics needed Narcan to revive him.

"What is happening? What is Narcan?" Vicky asks.

"Narcan is used to reverse the life-threatening effects of an opioid. It temporarily reverses the effects of the drug," the doctor explained. "We will keep him in the hospital until his parents get here."

Vicky and Drew decide to wait with Hunter until his parents arrive to explain the day's events. They all settle in for a long night as no one is looking forward to the parents' appearance.

"Since Hunter is staying in the hospital, I'll leave now and be back at 9:00 a.m. in the morning," Steele mumbled and realized he has to stop this bad habit.

CHAPTER 54

With reports of an increase in cyberattacks worldwide, which targets computer information systems, computer networks, and infrastructures, the State of Florida decides to be cautious. Therefore, it does audits of all their computers. The random audit reveals improper use of the state's computers. With that, the state auditors conducted an in-depth investigation, and they find the illegal software.

Steele learns that the audit showed someone installed a Virtual Private Network to hide their geographical location. He realized that the VPN encrypts all internet traffic and disguises online activity. VPN acts like a middle man between the devices and the internet. It encrypts all the data coming from one server before sending it over through another server in another location. A private VPN not only hides the actual Internet Protocol address but makes it seem like you are browsing from another site. So, it is possible to browse the dark web without detection.

The auditors explained to Steele that they logged into the personal profile on everyone's computer and found someone had installed the VPN software. They also noticed that someone had deleted the VPN software, but they found the evidence in the computer's recycle bin because the person had forgotten to empty the trash on his computer.

The chief explains that Steele has to find the culprit and learn why they put this illegal software on the computer.

"Okay, Chief. Can I use CSI Jack Wagner to help me with this case since he knows more about computers than I do?"

"Sure, use all the people and equipment you need to get to the bottom of this."

Steele and Wagner checked out the auditor's report, and it showed that someone had used Matt Lombardo's computer and had installed the software but forgot to empty the trash. They go over the evidence and decide their next step would be to do a background check and look at Lombardo's personnel file to learn more about him before going to his house.

Going over Lombardo's records, they find he was in foster care since birth and was moved to a new foster house every few months until he aged out of the system at eighteen.

His biological mother died in prison two years ago, which may have upset Lombardo. Otherwise, he doesn't have any family, according to the report.

"Well, it doesn't look like he had a good childhood. You knew him longer than I did. Does he seem like the kind of person to do something like this?" Steele asks.

"I don't know. Matt was a loner. He kept to himself and spent most of his time on the computer while at work. He never mentioned any family or even a girlfriend as long as I knew him. So, I really don't know anything about him."

They arrive at Lombardo's home and ring the doorbell. Although they can hear the television inside, no one answers the door. They see a wall of newspapers and disorder everywhere through the window. Concerned about his well-being, they kick in the door and find a small pathway into its interior, surrounded by stacks of magazines and newspapers almost reaching the ceiling.

They carefully walk over the scattered clothing, clutter, plastic bags, empty fast-food containers, debris, and junk throughout the house. Amid the rubble, they find Lombardo sitting in his overstuffed chair, staring blankly at the television.

"Matt, are you okay?" Wagner asks.

Surprised by his visitors, he tells them everything is okay, and they should leave.

"Matt, we have to talk to you. Are you okay?"

"Of course, I'm okay. Why wouldn't I be okay? What are you doing in my house?"

"You didn't answer the door, and we were concerned."

"I didn't hear you because I had my hearing aids turned down."

"I didn't know you had hearing aids," Wagner said.

Steele reads the Miranda warning, and Matt acknowledges he understands them.

"We are here because of the software you installed on your office computer. Can you tell us why you did that?" Steele asks.

"What are you talking about? I didn't do anything wrong."

"We have all the proof we need, and it shows it was your computer that you used to install illegal software on the state's computer."

"I didn't do anything wrong. I just needed to get on the dark web, and I don't own a computer, so I had to use the one in the office," Lombardo said.

"Why did you need to get on the dark web?"

"I had to find and buy a drug strong enough to kill someone quickly, and I found Carfentanil. It was perfect for my needs, but I didn't want anyone to know I was buying drugs on the dark web."

"What did you do with the drugs that you bought?" Steele asks.

"I sold it. I needed money to pay off my gambling debts so that they couldn't take everything away from me."

"Who bought the drugs from you?" Steele asks.

Lombardo explains how he met Pete at Tony's Pizza Parlor, and they started talking. After numerous meetings, Pete discovers where Lombardo worked and asks if he could find a drug that would make it easy to kill someone. After some research, Lombardo found the poison and sold it to Pete, but he never asked how he used the drugs.

"So, you bought illegal drugs on the dark web and sold them to Pete Rossi so he could kill someone? Is that right?" Steele asks.

"I sold them to Pete. He never told me his last name."

"We are talking about Pete, who works at Tony's Pizza Parlor. Is that correct?"

"That is what I said. So, then after I paid off my gambling debts, I just stayed home and started to save everything. I didn't want to lose anything anymore."

"What do you mean you didn't want to lose anything anymore?" Steele asks.

"For as long as I can remember, everybody would take my things. While in foster care, I never had anything that was mine because every time they moved me, they were always in a rush, and the caseworker didn't have time to let me take my things."

"Matt, have you been out of this house since you retired a couple of months ago?" Wagner asks.

"No, everything I need is delivered. I have no reason to go out. I like it here."

"We have to arrest you for installing illegal software on a state computer and buying illegal drugs on the dark web," Steele said as he put handcuffs on Lombardo.

Because of the condition of his house, his apparent mental distress, and obsessive-compulsive disorder, Lombardo is arrested and taken to the psychiatric ward of the hospital. He is Baker Acted and placed under a mandatory seventy-two-hour psychiatric evaluation. Steele will assign a uniform to him until he is cleared and taken to jail.

After the mandatory time, the doctor's evaluation of Lombardo reveals he is not mentally sound to stand trial and would not be able to help in his defense. So, he will stay in the psychiatric ward until he gets the help he needs.

CHAPTER 55

Mary and Jonathan Langford arrive at the hospital and loudly insist on seeing the doctor in charge.

"Where is my son?" Mary shouts.

Vicky hears her sister and rushes to hug her, but Mary pushes her away.

"I thought I could trust you to take care of my son," Mary said with her hands on her hips. "Now he is in the hospital because he overdosed, and it's all your fault. Where is my son? I want to see him now."

"Mary, it is so good to see you. After your long flight, your hair and makeup are still perfect, and your dress isn't wrinkled. You look like you are ready for a fashion photo shoot."

"Stop all your flattery. I'm still mad at you for not taking care of my son."

At this time, Steele walks in, introduces himself, and asks the parents to sit down so they can talk.

"I demand you tell me what is going on with my son and why are you here?" Mary asks with her arms folded in front of her.

"The DEA has enough evidence to show the young boys at the house and your son were selling drugs to the people in The Villages."

"No, that can't be true. Hunter would never sell drugs. I want to see my son right now," she demanded.

"DEA Agent Graham will be here shortly to arrest Hunter and take him to the Juvenile Detention Center. Where he will charge him with drug trafficking," Steele said.

The tension in the room intensifies as Mary and Vicky continue to bicker back and forth. Drew and Jonathan are trying to stop their wives from saying things they would later regret.

"This is all your fault, Vicky. You should have taken better care of him."

"This is not my fault. You are always traveling all over the world and leaving Hunter behind," Vicky said.

"You are just jealous of me because I have money and a son, and you don't have either one."

"Maybe if you didn't take the funds away from Hunter, he wouldn't need to start an illegal business to have money," Vicky said.

"This is all your fault Jonathan," Mary accuses. "You shouldn't have bought that house for him, just because he asked you. All this happened because of that house."

"Ladies, please settle down. You are not helping anything acting this way," Jonathan said as he put his arm around Mary, but she pulled away from his touch.

Agent Graham enters the waiting room during the shouting match between the two women.

"Mr. and Mrs. Langford, I want to tell you that your son is in a lot of trouble. He will need a good criminal defense attorney that specializes in drug cases. Although he is seventeen, the courts will probably charge him as an adult," Agent Graham said. "I'm here to take Hunter to Juvenile Detention. You may talk to him for a minute before we leave."

"Hunter, I am here for you if you need anything," Mary said, trying to hug her son.

"It's a little too late now, Mother. You were never there when I needed you. But I want to thank you, Aunt Vicky and Uncle Drew, for all your support over the years," Hunter said as Agent Graham took him away. "This is all your fault, Mother."

CHAPTER 56

After the confession of Matt Lombardo, Steele and Wagner make an appointment to visit Pete Rossi with Warren Wheeler, Rossi's attorney.

The three men sit around the square metal table in a private room reserved for lawyers in the county jail. They wait for the guard to bring in Rossi and remove his handcuffs and ankle restraints.

While Rossi is rubbing his sore wrists, his lawyer explains they are here to talk about the murders.

"I want you to know that I advise you not to say anything to the detective," Wheeler said.

"CSI Jack Wagner and I have talked to Matt Lombardo, and he explained in detail how he found the drug Carfentanil on the dark web and sold it to you," Steele said.

Against the advice of his lawyer, Rossi explains how he murdered the Palatka Pythons using the syringe filled with the lethal drug. He would lure them to the alley, jump out from the dumpster, and jab them in the butt.

"It was easy because they were so big that they didn't even see me until I stabbed them.

First, he describes his childhood as not good because he had an abusive father that beat him and constantly belittled him, so Rossi never finished school and knew he would never get a good job without a diploma.

After his father left, he moved in with his mother. Then he saw the help wanted sign in Tony's Pizza shop window, and he knew he could make enough money to keep his old car.

"Then I met Bette Thompson, and I knew as soon as I saw her that I wanted to marry her, but to do that, I had to make some money. So, I put an ad on the computer saying I would do anything for money."

"Where did you find a computer to use?" Steele asks.

"That was easy. There is an internet café just down the street. I would go there every day to see if anyone answered my ad. It didn't take long before someone contacted me, and I was in business."

"Do you know the name of the person that contacted you?"

"No. The person did everything on the computer, and they would pay me through Western Union. I just went to any Western Union locations and gave them the agreed-upon password, and I would get the money. After awhile, I bought my own computer so I wouldn't have to go to the café every day."

"How many people did you kill?"

"Don't answer the question. You give the police all the evidence needed to put you on death row. You need to stop right now," Wheeler said, slamming the table with his hand.

"It's all right, Mr. Wheeler. I know what I'm doing. In addition to some other legal jobs, I killed nine men. I killed six of them a couple of years ago and three just recently. I'm sorry I had to kill the men, but it was the only way I knew how to make money. After that, I had plenty of money to buy a house. Then I told Bette I loved her and had enough money to take care of us and the baby. Since they are both gone, I have no reason to live."

"The Boss told me each man had a lot of heroin to sell and a gun. What did you do with the drugs and guns?" Steele asks.

"I sold the guns with the gold necklaces to the pawnshop. That gave me a lot more money. The drugs I flushed down the toilet because I don't use drugs, and I didn't know what else to do with them."

"We appreciate you are giving us all the information on this case," Steele said.

After the interview, they thank Rossi while the guard handcuffs him and takes him back to his cell.

"I wonder why the pawnshop guy didn't tell me about buying the guns with the necklaces. Otherwise, that pretty much wraps up the case," Steele said.

CHAPTER 57

Steele calls Ashley and invites her to come to his office for the scoop he promised her.

"I can't believe you finally solved the Alleyway Murders. Tell me all the specifics."

Steele explains the complicated details. First, there was CSI Matt Lombardo. He bought the illegal drugs on the dark web and sold them to pizza delivery guy Pete Rossi. Rossi filled syringes with the illicit drug Carfentanil and injected the men in their buttocks.

"You have to give me more details. This isn't enough," Ashley said.

"Okay. It appeared Lombardo was having mental and gambling problems for some time before he retired a few months ago, but no one noticed anything since he is a loner. He is currently under arrest but is in the psychiatric ward until he is well enough to help in his defense."

"How did they meet? I need details," Ashley said.

"They met at Tony's Pizza shop. It seems Lombardo really liked pizza and spent a lot of time at Tony's Pizza Parlor and Rossi befriended him," Steele said.

"Okay, I got everything about Lombardo and Rossi. Now tell me about the guys that they murdered."

"This is the interesting part. All nine guys were from a gang called the Palatka Pythons. They had this tattoo of an ugly python snake going up against their right forearms with the snake's head tattooed on their neck. According to their boss, they wanted to expand their drug dealing area and thought the growing Villages would be a place to start. If the business looked promising, they planned to relocate here," Steele said.

Ashley is struggling to catch up with her notetaking of Steele's story.

"Did anyone tell you why Rossi killed the gang members?" she asked.

"It seemed a local gang called the Privileged, a group of young rich boys, were already selling drugs in The Villages. The boys hired Rossi to kill the gang members since they didn't want any competition. One of the boys put all this information on the computer, and if Rossi hadn't been careless and leave a partial fingerprint on the syringe, we probably would not have figured it out. We also had Lombardo give us some good information to help solve this. But, if Bette Thompson didn't get killed, Rossi wouldn't have gotten sloppy, and he would have kept killing out-of-town drug dealers."

"Wow. This is really complicated. I think I have everything I need for my story. Thanks for giving me the scoop over the other newspapers."

"You are quite welcome. I have a dinner date if you don't have any other questions," Steele said.

"Wait. What happened to Pete Rossi?"

"He is in the county jail waiting for his trial, and with the crowded court docket, it will probably be a year or two before they actually get to court. He's a nice guy that didn't get a break in life but managed to find someone to love."

"Okay. One more question. What about the rich boys? What happened to them?"

"Since they're minors, you can't put their names in the newspaper. They are being held in the Juvenile Detention Center, also awaiting trial. With the seriousness of their crime, the judge will probably charge them as adults. Okay, that's enough for now. If you have any other questions, you can call me tomorrow."

"Thanks for the information. This is going to be a great story," Ashley said.

Steele stops by Nancy's office to see if she is ready for dinner.

"I am ready to leave and can't wait for you to tell me all the details."

"No, I just finished telling Ashley Parker all the information about the Alleyway Murders, as she calls her story," Steele said.

Steele's phone rings before they can leave for dinner.

"I have to go to the county jail. Do you want to come along; then we can have dinner after?" Steele asks.

"That sounds good. Maybe then you can tell me who killed Bette Thompson while you're driving."

"You know we already charged Will Hudson with attempted murder. Since we don't have any fingerprints, witnesses, or other evidence on who actually smothered Thompson, it will become just another cold case. We'll probably never know the person that actually killed her," Steele said.

Steele goes into the county jail and learns that Pete Rossi hung himself in his cell. He was dead when the guards found him.

"Why wasn't he on suicide watch? I told you that the guards should be watching him when we brought him in," Steele said frustrated.

The guards don't offer any excuses. After getting the bad news, Steele takes Nancy back to her office.

"I'm sorry, Nancy, but I'm not really in a good mood right now with Rossi dead. Can I get a rain check on dinner?"

"Sure, Grant. I'll be ready for our dinner date anytime you're ready."